GW01451632

DOUBLE WEDDING RING

KRISTI LUNDRIGAN MYSTERY
BOOK THREE

DEBBIE MUMFORD

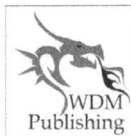

WDM
Publishing

COPYRIGHT

DOUBLE WEDDING RING
Copyright © 2024 by Debbie Mumford
Published by WDM Publishing
Cover and Layout copyright © 2024 by WDM Publishing
Cover designed by Getcovers

PRAISE FOR DEBBIE MUMFORD

Praise for *Delectable Mountain Quilting*:

LW from Amazon: Five stars: *"Will read more of the series. Love quilting and related stuff. Story was gripping and well constructed."*

———

Jean from Amazon: Five stars: *"I enjoyed the easy read. A nice story with likable people. I used to quilt, so I understand the value of the antique quilt."*

———

Praise for *In a Pickle*:

Quilter from Amazon: Five stars: *"I'm a quilter and throughly enjoyed this story. I like a good series like this second book."*

———

Norrine B from Amazon: Five stars: *"Kept you on the edge of your seat. Good book for a snowy day in front of a fireplace with a warm beverage."*

———

Praise for *Second Sight*:

Bookgirl from Amazon: Five stars: "A lost love, a new love, psychic magic, a murder and a tiger! Wow. I loved this book. It was fast paced and easy to read. I got caught up in the "I'll just read one more chapter" syndrome and lost a bit of sleep but it was worth it. I hope Ms. Mumford writes more in this world. I love these characters."

———

Dragon Slayer from Amazon: Five stars: "I liked the characters and the story line. For those that love a mystery and a good romance along with the paranormal, this book is for you."

———

Praise for *Sorcha's Heart*

Katie from Goodreads: Five stars: 'This story was fantastic...I strongly recommend anyone who likes paranormal dragon stories read this. Best prequel ever. Off to look for more by this author."

———

Old Ozark Gal from Amazon: Five stars: "...for those who enjoy a sizzling relationship without the graphic descriptions of what body part goes where, this is an excellent book. So what are you waiting for? Go read it!"

———

Karyn-Anne from Amazon: Five stars: "The romantic scenes were full of passion and heat, but not graphic or explicit. I really, really enjoyed this novella … Very highly recommended!"

———

Ahmari from Amazon: Five stars: "This book is very well written … I liked it so much I purchased the sequel! … a unique idea for a fantasy and told in a delightful manner. I look forward to reading more from this author."

———

Praise for *Her Highland Laird*:

Katharina from Amazon: Five stars: "I'm normally not someone who reads romance novels, but … I stumbled over Debbie Mumford's Romance stories. This one was an absolute treat. Not only did it depict the life in 15th century correctly (well researched for such a short story), it evokes emotion very well … I'll definitely read more by this author."

———

Tony from Amazon: Five stars: "Very interesting story. With some suspense and an interesting thread of love."

SATURDAY MORNING

Kristiana Lundrigan, Kristi to her friends and family, sailed into *Roasted Beans*, her signature ankle length patchwork skirt swirling around her legs. Her best friend, Stacy Akins Robards, waved to her from a two-top table framed by the large window that fronted Main Street. Smiling, Kristi nodded and, inhaling the rich aromas of freshly brewed coffee, flavorful teas, and the sugary sweetness of delectable baked goods, wove through the remaining tables to reach her friend.

"Thanks for meeting me this morning," she said as she draped her embroidered denim shoulder bag across the back of a chair and settled down, unzipping her down jacket and pulling the knit hat from her head. Finger-combing her shoulder length blonde hair, she winced as her ring caught in a tangle.

"What?" asked Stacy, concern shadowing her gaze.

Kristi laughed. "It's nothing. I'm just not used to wearing this ring yet."

Stacy squealed and held out her hand. "Let me see it!" Where-upon Kristi obliged by placing her left hand in Stacy's outstretched right. A stunning emerald cut diamond solitaire sparkled on Kristi's ring finger. Set in a simple white gold band, the stone was simply brilliant.

"That is a gorgeous ring, Kristi. I can't believe you and Jason waited so long to get it."

Kristi raised her hand to study the solitaire. "It is beautiful, isn't it?" She twisted her hand back forth, admiring the way the light danced across the facets. "It's nothing like my first ring." She dropped her hand to the table and turned her attention to Stacy. "That's really what took so long. Neither Jason nor I wanted to start our new engagement with leftovers from our failed marriage, but we couldn't decide on how to handle the old rings."

She paused for a moment when she noticed a server headed their direction carrying two steaming mugs. "Did you order for me?"

"Sure did," Stacy said with a nod. "I know what you like, a nice hot cup of chai."

The server arrived and placed the mugs on the table. "Coffee for you, Stacy, and chai for Kristi."

"Thanks, Jenny," Stacy said. "Perfect as always."

The dark-haired server smiled and said, "Let me know if you need anything else," before she turned to go.

Kristi took a sip of her chai, savoring the rich taste of black tea subtly spiced and fragrant with cinnamon, black pepper, and ginger, and just the right amount of creamy sweetness.

"Okay," Stacy said. "Hot beverage break is over; back to the story of that gorgeous ring."

Kristi saluted. "Aye, aye, Captain!" She took another sip of chai, placed the mug on the table and curled her fingers around its warmth. "Well, while two people who have been married before getting engaged is nothing new, two people who were formerly married *to each other* getting back together is a bit more... unusual.

Stacy nodded and sipped her coffee.

"I mean, I still had my original engagement ring, as well as my old wedding band. So did Jason. But neither of us wanted to use any of those rings. Too much baggage."

Stacy leaned forward. "What did you decide to do?"

"We visited Mr. Kauffman." She picked up her cup and sipped. *Kauffman's Jewelry* was the only jewelry store in Garnet Gateway, so the choice hardly registered as a surprise.

"And?"

"And, after telling Mr. Kauffman our story and showing him the old rings, he suggested we sell him all three and put the money towards a new ring."

"And did you? You didn't go to Billings and shop around?"

Kristi shook her head. "Nope. No Billings. We both wanted to keep the cash in the local community. Besides, we like Mr. Kauffman."

Stacy flexed her fingers in a *show me* gesture and Kristi placed her left hand on the table. The solitaire sparkled in the sunlight.

Stacy gazed at the diamond and sighed. "Did Mr. Kauffman have that on hand?"

Kristi's expression softened as she gazed at the ring. "No. We looked at everything he had in the shop, but nothing spoke to us." She glanced up and met Stacy's gaze with a wry smile. "If we'd found something in stock, I'd have had my ring months ago. No, Jason sketched out what he thought we wanted and I added my idea about the white gold setting and Mr. Kauffman went to work contacting his friends in the business to see what they could come up with.

"Over the last few months we saw some beautiful rings— folks sent him pictures for us to look at— but it wasn't until we saw this one that we both knew that was *our* ring."

"Well, it was certainly worth the wait," Stacy said. "Did the sale of those other rings cover the cost?"

Kristi shrugged. "No idea. Jason swore Mr. Kauffman to secrecy about the finances. But Jason seems proud and pleased, so I'm just going to assume that all is well."

Stacy nodded. "Good for him, and good for you." Picking up her coffee cup, she took another sip. "So. Now. When's the wedding?"

Kristi grinned. "A week from today! Want to help?"

Stacy nearly spit that sip of coffee on the table, but she forced herself to swallow. "Seriously? A week from today?"

"Yup. Both sets of parents are coming for Thanksgiving, so we're going to save them another trip and just get married on the Saturday after Turkey Day."

"But… but… there are a million things to arrange! Have you been planning this for months and just haven't told me?"

"Nope," Kristi said with a giggle. "We picked up the ring on Thursday afternoon, looked at each other, and said *let's get married*! So that's what we're doing."

"But…"

Kristi waved away Stacy's concerns. "No worries. It's going to be a very small, very informal wedding. Just you and Mark to stand up for us, our parents, a few of Jason's staff from the sheriff's office, and a few of my fellow quilters. We may even hold it in our living room."

"What about a reception?"

"I'm going to swing by *Rizzoli's* today and ask Mama if we can do something there."

Stacy studied her friend's face, then grabbed Kristi's hand and said, "Let me do that. I have an idea. Be thinking about what kind of flowers you want and your favorite cake flavor. I'll handle the rest." She bit her lip and stared off into space for a moment. Then her eyes went wide and her mouth dropped open. "A dress! What about a dress?"

"Oh," Kristi said quietly. "Hadn't thought about that yet. I'm sure I've got something that will work."

"Oh, no. You're not just pulling something out of your closet for your wedding." Giving a determined nod, Stacy drained her coffee cup and gathered her coat and purse. "Come on. Finish that chai and put your jacket on. We're going to *Delectable Mountain Quilting*. Your staff needs to get in on this planning."

Kristi gulped her rapidly cooling chai, grabbed her things, and stood. "They do? Why? They're already working on a Double Wedding Ring quilt for us. I can't ask them to do anything else!"

Stacy was already nearly to the door. She turned and nodded briskly. "Trust me. They'll definitely want to help with this, too!"

———

SHERIFF JASON REYNOLDS strode into the single story white stucco building that housed the sheriff's department. Nodding to the deputy on duty at the high wooden counter that separated the public portion of the room from the area where his staff worked, he headed for the door to his office.

"Morning, Sheriff," called Clara, his dispatcher and sometimes secretary. "What are you doing here on a Saturday? You're supposed to be off duty."

Jason paused with his hand on the doorknob and smiled. "Too many things to do, Clara. You do remember I'm going to be gone for a while, don't you?"

She laughed. "Of course I do. It's not every day that our sheriff gets married and goes off on his honeymoon!"

"Good thing, too," he said with mock seriousness. "This place might fall down around our ears if I took too much time off."

"Hah!" exclaimed Janet Millson. His chief deputy and right-hand woman had stepped to Clara's desk just in time to hear his facetious comment. "We'll limp along just fine in your absence, thank you very much."

Jason saluted the two women. "I know you will." Pasting a scowl on his face, he added, "And neither of you had better be limping when I get back."

Both women laughed.

"When do we get our invitations to the big event?" Janet called as he opened the door and stepped into his office.

He waved the question away. "Talk to Kristi. I've got a county to keep safe."

Closing the door behind himself, he glanced around his small office. It wasn't much to look at— a little on the dingy side, with pale green walls, an old-fashioned teacher's desk, a pair of gray metal filing cabinets, and an overflowing bookshelf— but it was his and he was proud to occupy it. Proud to be trusted enough by the citizens of Garnet County, Montana to hold this elected office.

He pulled off his shearling sheepskin coat and hung it and his Stetson on the coat rack beside the window. Moving to his desk he settled into the ancient rolling desk chair and pulled over a stack of paperwork. He planned to be off duty as of the end of the day on Wednesday and he had a lot of work to get through first.

Smiling to himself, he considered the week ahead. His parents, as well as Kristi's, would be arriving on Tuesday. Thursday was Thanksgiving, and on Saturday... his grin brightened... on Saturday he and Kristi would be married.

Again.

He'd been a fool to cheat on her last time, but he'd learned his lesson. No way would he ever do anything to jeopardize their relationship again. He'd had to work too hard to win her back to ever lose this second marriage. Kristi was his one and only, and he knew it to the depths of his being.

He was incredibly lucky to have won this second chance.

Jason could hardly wait for their honeymoon. He'd only managed a week off, but he planned to take full advantage of those uninterrupted days... and nights. Kristi didn't know where he was taking her, but he was absolutely positive she was going to love their destination.

Sighing, he pushed thoughts of the honeymoon away and turned his attention to the first paper on the stack in front of him. It was important to him to leave his department in good order while he was gone, so he put his head down and got to work. He was nearly halfway through the stack when a soft knock sounded at his office door.

"Come," he called.

The door opened and Clara peered around the edge. "Excuse me, Sheriff," she said, "but don't you have a lunch date with your lovely fiancé?"

Jason glanced at his watch, saw that it was half past eleven, and straightened the remaining papers in the stack before rising.

"I certainly do," he said with a grin. "Thanks for the reminder, Clara."

Nodding, she said, "No problem. Have a nice time." With that she disappeared from the doorway.

Jason followed, grabbing his coat and hat and shrugging into them as he prepared to leave his office. Time to concentrate on Kristi, the love of his life!

He stopped when his cell phone rang. Frowning, he accepted the call and said, "Sheriff Reynolds."

2

SATURDAY MIDMORNING

Stacy was absolutely right. Kristi's staff definitely wanted to get in on the wedding planning. So much so that Ruby Andrews, who'd been the on-duty clerk, had called in Mattie Stebbings, as well as Kristi's bookkeeper, DeAnna Waters. Mattie had even insisted on calling Eula Gibbs, a retired grandmother who sold her baby quilts on consignment and helped out when needed. The only person they hadn't called was Andrea Jansson, but only because the vivacious young woman was in the middle of classes at her community college in Billings.

Once everyone had gathered, oohed and aahed over the ring, and turned the sign in the front window to *Closed*, they got down to work, poo-pooing the idea that making a quilt for Kristi and Jason precluded them helping with the actual wedding.

Kristi's head swam with the plans her friends were making on her behalf. Sure, it was going to be a small wedding, but with all five of Kristi's staff, both sets of parents, Stacy and Mark, plus at least five of Jason's people, they were nearing twenty bodies. Which was probably at least ten more than Kristi's living room could comfortably accommodate.

Stacy said she'd take care of the venue for both the ceremony and the reception. Kristi wasn't to give it another thought!

Eula volunteered her garden group to take care of the flowers. They'd make sure Kristi had a beautiful bouquet even though Thanksgiving week was late in Montana's growing season. Eula and her friends would also provide several centerpieces for the reception.

DeAnna offered to contact her brother-in-law to see if he was available to photograph the wedding. She assured Kristi that if Kevin took the assignment, he'd give them his "friends and family" discount.

That left Mattie and Ruby with the task of helping Kristi pick a wedding gown.

"I can't wait!" Ruby squealed. "This is going to be so much fun!"

"I'll make an appointment with Delilah Reed," Mattie said. "She owns *Delilah's Dresses* and will have the best selection in town. She's a friend of mine and will be happy to do an after-hours meeting so we won't have to close the shop. Plus, we'll have the store to ourselves and won't be interrupted."

Kristi bit her lip. "Okay, but keep in mind, you two, this is a second wedding. And a small one. I don't want some over-the-top pure white wedding dress. I'll be looking for something simple that can be worn again. Got it?"

Ruby and Mattie nodded.

"Simple, but elegant," Mattie agreed.

"Not white," Ruby said, "but maybe cream or... ooo, gold would be beautiful with your coloring and a perfect match for fall flowers."

"We'll see," Kristi said noncommittally.

"All right, everyone," Stacy said, grabbing their attention with a clap. "We all have our assignments, so let's get to it." She turned and grinned at Kristi. "Besides, I can see that our bride-to-be is getting antsy to reopen the shop."

Kristi laughed. "She is indeed! Thanks everyone. I really appreciate all of your help. It's going to be a much classier wedding than it would've been if I'd tried to do everything on my own."

Eula paused in pulling on her down jacket. "Don't you worry, dear. We've got your back."

"Definitely," Mattie agreed.

And with that, the impromptu planning session broke up. Stacy, Eula, DeAnna, and Mattie headed out the door, while Ruby turned the sign back to *Open*. Kristi wandered into the break room, sat down at her desk and pulled her laptop computer out of the drawer. She had a few minutes before Jason was scheduled arrive for their lunch date, so she might as well give some thought to ordering some new bolts of fabric. Checking her notes, she saw that the flannel backing fabrics had been selling well. Time to see what new patterns were being offered.

3

SATURDAY LATE MORNING

Jason frowned as he accepted the call on his cell phone. He didn't want to talk to anyone; he wanted to take Kristi to lunch. But he was the sheriff of Garnet County. He had responsibilities.

"Sheriff Reynolds," he said, hoping his voice didn't carry too much annoyance.

"Well," said a familiar voice, "don't you sound official!"

"Dad." he exclaimed, closing the door to his office to maintain a bit of privacy. "Why are you calling? Is anything wrong? Is Mom okay?"

"Relax, Sheriff," his father said with a laugh. "Just because no one in Montana calls you unless it's an emergency doesn't mean your dear old dad can't call just to chat with his favorite son."

"Your only son, you mean."

"True, but you're definitely my favorite young man."

Jason slumped into his desk chair, still wearing his sheepskin coat. He loved his dad, but the man's timing sucked. Jason had a date with Kristi!

"The question stands, Dad. If nothing is wrong, why the call. You're not the chatty type."

Dad sighed, but Jason could hear the amusement in the sound. "Fine. Down to business. Your mother wanted me to make sure you had our schedule and flight numbers. I think she's worried about flying into Montana this late in the year."

Jason laughed out loud. "Right. She's worried about the weather! Dad, you two lived here for more than twenty years."

"Exactly," Dad agreed. "She knows how unpredictable Montana's winters can be."

"It's late November, not early January. The weather will be cold but not freezing."

"Yep. That's what I figure, but she'll be glad to hear you agree. Okay, got something to write on?"

"Always. Give me the info when you're ready."

Jason's dad filled him in on airlines, flight numbers, connecting flights, and when they'd arrive in Billings. "Now, will you be able to pick us up, or should we rent a car and drive down?"

"I'll pick you up." Jason paused a moment and thought about that statement. "At least, I will if I can. If something comes up, I'll send one of my deputies to retrieve you. But you definitely don't need to rent a car."

"What about getting back to Billings after the wedding? You and Kristi had better not be around to drive us to the airport."

Jason grinned though he knew his dad couldn't see him. "Don't worry. We won't. But our friends, Mark and Stacy, have agreed to make sure you and the Lundrigans don't miss your flights."

"Excellent," his dad said. "Well, I know you're busy, so I won't keep you, but your mother and I are looking forward to seeing you and Kristi, as well as her parents. See you in a few days."

"See you soon, Dad. Give Mother a hug for me and tell her not to worry. Everything will be fine."

"Love you, Son."

"Love you too, Dad!"

Smiling, Jason ended the call, stood, and strode to the office door. He just had enough time to get to *Delectable Mountain Quilting* and collect Kristi for their lunch date.

Life was good.

4

SATURDAY NOON

Kristi glanced up from her computer spreadsheet when she heard the bell over the front door chime. Jason strode into the shop, touched the brim of his Stetson in salute to Ruby, and made his way to the break room where Kristi waited. Taking a moment to appreciate her fiancé's physique, she sighed dreamily.

The sheriff was an undeniably handsome man, especially when Montana's famously cold weather called for that shearling sheepskin coat. Between that, his Stetson, and his cowboy boots, he looked every inch the western sheriff. His wide shoulders, strong jaw, and steely gray eyes made him a formidable opponent for miscreants, but Kristi was particularly fond of the wavy chestnut hair currently hidden under his Stetson. Of course, the way he filled out his khaki uniform shirt and well-worn blue jeans didn't hurt either.

No doubt about it, she was a lucky woman!

"Hey there, gorgeous," he said, his voice almost purring. "Ready for lunch?"

Kristi grinned. "Definitely. Just let me save this spreadsheet and put the computer away."

A very few moments later she stood and grabbed her down jacket and knit hat, but before she could put either on Jason pulled her into a tight embrace and kissed her soundly.

"There," he murmured as he released her. "Now I can make it through lunch."

She giggled and swatted him playfully on the arm. "Where are we going?"

"I thought we'd head over to the Garnet Gateway Inn," he said as he helped her into her coat. "They have a nice lunch buffet. Then, if we have time, maybe take a walk through Riverside Park."

"That sounds wonderful. Let's do it."

Besides being delicious, lunch was great fun. The buffet included an extensive selection, but Kristi settled on a fairly mundane choice, a slice of pepperoni pizza and a small salad. Jason was evidently feeling more adventurous. He paired a hearty serving of hot wings with macaroni and cheese, and topped his plate off with a ham sandwich on rye.

No doubt about it, the man could eat!

While they polished off their respective meals, Kristi told him about her morning and the plans her friends were making for the wedding.

Jason looked a bit shocked, but held his peace until they left the inn and were meandering through the park.

"So," he began, "not to disparage Stacy's taste, but do you really trust her to choose our venue? I mean, she's great and I know she's a close friend, but I thought we were going to do this at home. You know, keep it small."

Kristi tucked her gloved hand in the crook of his sheepskin clad arm and leaned against his side. "I know and I agree. But Stacy's got a point. We've got about twenty people that we want to invite and that's pushing it for our living room. It'd be different if we could move into the backyard, but at this time of year, that's just not practical."

He nodded. "True."

"And I've stressed that we don't want a fancy place, just somewhere our guests can assemble comfortably." They strolled quietly beside Garnet Creek for a few moments, gradually angling toward the carousel at the center of the park. "Speaking of guests, we need to sit down and finalize our list so I can send out invitations."

He stopped, looking startled. "Invitations? You're not planning to have *Paradise Printers* print them are you? I'm not sure there's enough time."

She laughed. "No. Nothing that fancy. I'm just going to buy some simple cards and handwrite them, once we settle on a venue and time, of course." They started walking again. The carousel was just a few steps away now.

"Okay," Jason said. "We'll make an evening of it. You write the cards; I'll address the envelopes."

"That works," she said, smiling. "Shall we sit for a moment?"

They'd reached the carousel. The gayly painted mechanical ride had been the centerpiece of Riverside Park since the park was established in the early 1950s. Along with the fanciful horses, the ride featured benches built to resemble Roman chariots, each with "reins" leading to two of the prancing horses. Mirrors ringed with colorful lights decorated the central column housing the machinery that made the whole thing go around.

Of course, this late in the season, the carousel stood quiet and unused. No flashing lights. No horses leaping and running. Just a stationary device that invited visitors to step onto the platform and wander among the chariots and horses.

When Kristi and Jason stepped onto the carousel, Jason immediately settled onto one of the chariot benches. But Kristi chose to stroll among the horses, petting noses and murmuring greetings to each one. After all, the horses were old friends. She'd enjoyed this carousel every summer since she'd moved to Garnet Gateway.

She was on the opposite side of the ride from Jason when she saw the man. He sat slumped on a chariot bench and seemed to be sleeping. Her instinct was to call for Jason, but the fellow seemed harmless, so she continued greeting the painted horses. When she came even with the man, she prepared to greet him as well, but one look told her he wouldn't respond. Would never respond to a greeting again.

His face was slack, eyes open but unseeing, and the front of his ranch coat was covered in blood.

"Jason!" Kristi screamed. "Jason, come quickly!" She stepped back until she could no longer see the man's face and all the blood, then closed her eyes and leaned against the nearest carousel horse as Jason's footsteps pounded ever closer.

He reached her side, grabbed her arm and turned her to face him. "What is it? What's wrong?"

She closed her eyes and gestured toward the chariot bench and managed to choke out a few words. "Th... that man. H... he's dead."

———

AFTER DOING a quick check on the body to verify Kristi's statement that the man was dead, Jason gathered his fiancé in his arms and held her tightly. The unknown man could wait for another few minutes. Kristi couldn't. She'd had a shock; her body trembled in his arms.

If only he hadn't sat down on that damn carousel bench! He should've stayed with her. He knew how much she enjoyed greeting each of the horses and couldn't imagine any harm in it, so he'd let his guard down.

Damn it!

He shouldn't have let her find that body alone. She'd had too much of that. First Stebbings, then the poisoning at the fair, and now this. He blew out the breath he hadn't realized he was holding and pulled her tighter against his chest. He wanted to protect her so badly… and he'd failed again.

When her trembling calmed, Jason eased her back so he could study her face. Her eyes were dark with shock, but she managed a weak smile. He nodded, released her, and led her around the curve of the carousel to the other side. Away from the body and the activity that he would soon instigate. Installing her on the chariot bench he'd occupied earlier. He kissed her gently on the forehead and said, "You'll be all right, sweetheart. Just sit here and rest while I call this in."

She closed her eyes and nodded. "I'm fine," she said, though she was very pale and her voice sounded weak. "Do what you need to do. I'm not going anywhere."

He patted her arm, then stood, moved a few paces away, and pulled out his cell phone. When Clara answered, he glanced back to make sure Kristi was okay, before moving around the curve of the carousel toward the dead man.

"Clara, we've got a body in Riverside Park. Send Eric and Roger, and Janet if she's available. I'll be waiting at the carousel."

"Right away, Sheriff," she answered, sounding every bit as capable and efficient as he knew she was. "Anything else.?"

"Yes," Jason responded, his mind clicking through the necessities of a murder investigation. "Get ahold of the coroner, Sean Bowman, and ask him to arrange for an ambulance. And to come himself."

"Will do."

"Oh," he added, a last minute thought coming to mind. "Ask Eric Lawson to make a stop on his way over..." and he quickly detailed his request. He could almost hear Clara nodding along.

"I'll take care of it, sir."

With the wheels in motion for his department's investigation, Jason ended the call and placed his cell phone in his coat pocket. Next, he unbuttoned his sheepskin coat long enough to pull the ever-present notepad and pen from his khaki colored uniform shirt pocket. Ready to record his observations, he approached the body.

The man was slouched in the corner of the chariot bench, his eyes open, but glazed in death. He wore a charcoal colored wool ranch coat with a lambskin collar. A serviceable outer garment worn by many men in the area. Blue jeans and scuffed cowboy boots. No hat or gloves. He appeared to be around thirty years old, with dirty blond hair in need of a trim and the scruff of a beard just darkening his cheeks and chin. His eyes looked to have been blue, but were whitening in death.

Jason didn't recognize him, but someone would. Garnet Gateway was a small town at heart and even the outlying ranches would soon hear of the death. If any ranch hands were missing, Jason or one of his staff would hear about it.

Without touching the body, Jason made note of the lethal wound. Blood soaked the front of the man's coat from what looked like a pair of knife wounds. One near the belly and one in the chest. Sean Bowman would determine the time and exact cause of death, but Jason couldn't imagine that this wouldn't be determined to be murder.

He shook his head, wondering what the man had done to deserve this violent end. Well, he'd figure it out. He always did.

He was just starting to walk a grid around the body looking for the murder weapon when his back-up arrived.

Janet and Roger stopped on the winter-brown grass just beyond the carousel.

"Hey, Sheriff," Janet called. "What have we got?"

Jason glanced up, nodded, and stepped off the carousel to brief his deputies. He'd barely finished when the ambulance pulled into the parking lot and Sean Bowman emerged and strode to join them. Since they knew they weren't dealing with an emergency, the med techs took their time, gathering the stretcher and body bag and following at a sedate pace.

Sean joined Jason and his deputies, nodded to them and said, "Where's the body?"

Jason swept an arm toward the carousel and led Sean to the dead man.

Sean knelt beside the body, checked for pulse and respiration, then did a cursory examination of the wound. Opening the ranch jacket, he found the man's wallet in an inside pocket and handed it to Jason.

Opening the wallet, Jason flipped through the contents. "We've got a name: Ray Carrick, and he wasn't robbed. There's a couple hundred dollars in here."

Sean nodded. "Taking the cold weather into account, I'd say he's been here for seven or eight hours."

"That would put time of death at around five this morning," Jason said.

Sean looked up, locking gazes with Jason. "That'll give you a place to start, but don't take it as gospel. I'll know more after the autopsy." He shook his head. "Definitely murder... which is becoming all too common around here. At least Kristi wasn't involved this time."

Jason gave him a wan smile and gestured toward the other side of the carousel. "She's over there. She found the body."

Sean closed his eyes and sighed. "Sheriff, your fiancé seems to be a magnet for trouble."

"Tell me about it," Jason muttered.

5

SATURDAY EARLY AFTERNOON

In what might have been minutes, or possibly hours— Kristi's mind wasn't firmly fixed in the here and now— deputies pulled into the parking lot which she could just see from where she sat huddled on the carousel bench. An ambulance followed soon after, probably bringing the coroner. Kristi shivered. She couldn't get the image of the dead man out of her mind. All that blood!

She glanced away when she saw the corpse being carted off a few minutes later, now safely hidden from sight in a black body bag. She was so focused on that black bag that she jumped when a hand touched her shoulder.

"Sorry," said a man's voice beside her. "Didn't mean to startle you."

Turning, she saw an earnest young man in a uniform similar to Jason's, official khaki colored shirt with a badge pinned above the pocket under an unfastened sheepskin jacket, blue denim jeans, and a Stetson cowboy hat.

"That's okay," she said. "Not your fault; I'm just a little jumpy."

She frowned. "I'm sorry. I know we've met, but I'm not coming up with your name."

"Lawson. Eric Lawson."

"That's right." She nodded. "You helped with the Studebakker case last summer."

"Yep, that was me." He smiled and held out an insulated paper cup with a white sipping lid. "The sheriff sent me over with this. He thought you might need a hot drink."

Taking the cup, she nodded. "Thank you, and thank Jason for me as well."

Deputy Lawson touched the brim of his hat, turned and strode away around the curve of the carousel.

Kristi took a careful sip, expecting coffee. Instead, she tasted the rich, creamy, spices of her favorite drink, hot chai. Trust Jason to know what she needed. Closing her eyes, she savored the familiar flavors and the much needed warmth. After a few swallows, she roused herself from the numb detachment she'd fallen into and stood. She'd seen the body taken away, she should be safe to go in search of Jason.

Jason must have heard her footsteps as he glanced over his shoulder as she rounded the curve of the carousel. He nodded at something Deputy Millson said, then turned and walked to Kristi.

"How are you?" he asked, placing his hands on her shoulders and gazing into her eyes.

"Better," she said. "That cup of chai really helped."

He nodded. "I'm glad."

"Do you need me here for anything?"

He studied her before shaking his head. "Not really. I'll need a statement eventually, but that can wait since I was on the scene. Why?"

She glanced toward the chariot bench where his deputies were gathering evidence before meeting his gaze.

"I need to get back to the shop," she said quietly, "but if you need me to stay, I will. I'll just call Ruby and let her know what's going on."

"Not necessary," he said, putting an arm around her shoulders and turning her away from the crime scene. "Do you want me to have Deputy Lawson walk you to the shop?"

She shook her head and smiled up at him. "No, Sheriff. I can find my way all by myself."

He grinned. "I know you can." He paused before adding, "But text me when you're back in the shop. Just so I'll know you're safe."

Placing a hand on his cheek, she kissed him lightly. "Will do. See you at home later."

As she walked back to *Delectable Mountain Quilting*, Kristi realized she hadn't asked if Jason had been able to identify the man. Not that it mattered. Kristi was unlikely to have known him. The memory of another man she'd found dead floated across her mind's eye. She hadn't thought Gary Stebbings had anything to do with her either, but he'd turned out to be Mattie's husband.

Garnet Gateway was a small town, but it was the hub of a ranching community. Its people were connected in unexpected ways. She sincerely hoped this dead man was totally unrelated to her own circle of friends and acquaintances.

6

SATURDAY MIDAFTERNOON

Once Jason received Kristi's text that she was safely back at the quilt shop, he called Clara.

"Garnet County Sheriff's Department," she said, answering after a single ring.

"Hey, Clara. It's me."

"What can I do for you, Sheriff?"

Jason glanced at the crime scene. His deputies had the area roped off with yellow tape and were busy collecting evidence and dusting for prints. They knew what they were doing and Janet Millson, his chief deputy, could be trusted to keep the situation under control. He didn't need to be here right now.

"We've established the victim's identity. Ray Carrick." He gave Clara the information, including address, listed on the man's driver's license. "I need you to find out his next of kin so I can notify them."

"Of course. Anything else?"

Jason thought for a moment, then shook his head though Clara wouldn't see the motion. "No. Not at the moment. I imagine the crew will be back to the office soon. Janet will direct the work-up on the man. She may have an additional research assignment for you."

"Fine. I'll call you back with the information on next of kin. Shouldn't take long."

"Thanks, Clara."

Jason ended the call, then turned to find Janet Millson. He caught her eye and she strode across the carousel to join him.

"You've got everything under control here," he said when she stood by his side. "I'm going to head over to the address listed on Carrick's driver's license. Clara is researching his next of kin. If I don't find a wife at his address, I'll make the notification as soon as Clara gets back to me."

Janet grimaced. "Better you than me."

With a shrug, Jason turned and walked away. "Not pleasant," he said over his shoulder, "but it has to be done."

A few minutes later, Jason parked his white Trail Blazer across the street from a neat, two-story board and batten home. A paved walk ran from the street to the front porch and Jason noted the remains of well-tended garden beds lining both sides of the walk. The Carrick home would have flowers to welcome guests in the spring and summer. He sighed. This didn't look like a bachelor's home. He hated ruining a wife's life by informing her she was now a widow.

Steeling himself, he was just about to climb out of his vehicle when his cell rang. Glancing at the display, he saw that the call was from Clara.

"Hey, Clara," he said as he accepted the call. "What have you got for me?"

"Ray Carrick was an auto mechanic and he worked at Kecskés Auto Repair. His next of kin is his wife, Denise, of the address listed on his license. He also has a brother, Davey Carrick, who works for your friend Mark Robards. Parents, James and Olivia Carrick, live in Billings. I have their phone number if you want it."

Jason nodded to himself. He could wait to notify the parents until he got back to the office, but it wouldn't hurt to have the information now. "Text the parents' number to me. And good work, Clara. I'm about to make the notification to the wife now."

She sighed. "Good luck, Sheriff," she said, then added softly, "Poor woman."

Jason couldn't agree more. Ending the call, he exited the Trail Blazer and walked across the street. He hated this part of his job.

———

An hour later Jason considered his next move as he walked from the Carrick home to his Trail Blazer. Denise Carrick hadn't been able to give him any possible motives for her husband's murder. Of course, she was also in shock. Perhaps after she'd had time to think, she'd remember something that might send the investigation in a new direction. At the moment, he'd accomplished nothing other than delivering news that left the woman devastated.

He hoped his deputies were making more progress than he was.

Opening the driver's side door, Jason climbed into his vehicle, but instead of inserting the key and starting the engine, he pulled his notebook from his pocket. Reviewing the few notes he had on

Ray Carrick, he noted that he had a brother. Davey Carrick. If the deceased had been in trouble or into shady business dealings, maybe he'd confided in his brother.

After a moment's consideration, he pulled his cell phone from his pocket and called Mark Robards. Davey Carrick might be more forthcoming if his boss was along for the interview.

"Robards Construction." Mark's deep baritone voice was all business when he accepted the call.

"Hey, Mark. It's Jason. Have you got a minute?"

"For you, Sheriff? Of course."

"Is Davey Carrick still working for you?"

Mark hesitated a moment before saying, "He is. Is he in trouble?"

"Not that I'm aware of, but I do need to talk to him. Do you know where he is right now?"

"No. We're waiting for delivery on a set of windows, so I gave the guys the afternoon off. No sense in paying them to sit around twiddling their thumbs. I think Davey and Jack Ryder were planning to saddle up and head into the 'Sorkees. They could be anywhere by now."

"I see. Well that complicates things."

"What's up, Jason?"

"Carrick's brother, Ray, was murdered. We found the body earlier and I need to interview Davey Carrick. See if he knows anything about any trouble Ray might have been into."

Mark gave a low whistle. "I'm sorry to hear that. I didn't know Ray, but Davey's a good kid and a hard worker."

Jason thought for a moment, then asked his friend a question. "Look, this isn't normal procedure, but if I manage to find Davey and set up a meeting, would you be willing to come along? He might feel more at ease, more willing to share, with a friendly face in the room."

"I could do that. Especially if you can make it tomorrow. My crew doesn't work on Sunday."

"I'll see what I can do. Thanks, Mark."

Ending the call, Jason started the engine and pulled away from the curb. Time to get back to the office and find out what his deputies had learned.

7

SATURDAY EVENING

Kristi had been home for several hours before Jason arrived. She'd made it back to the shop without incident, texted Jason as requested, then collapsed into the comfortable overstuffed chair they'd placed near the front window for use by husbands who accompanied their wives shopping. After all, comfortable men were less likely to rush their wives.

Ruby, noticing Kristi's pallor, had fixed her a cup of tea before worming the story of the dead man at the carousel out of her. After that, there had been no reasoning with the woman. Ruby had insisted on bundling Kristi back into her down jacket and sending her home.

"We're not busy today," Ruby had said, "and if we get busy, I'll call Mattie. Now go home. Take a hot soak or a nap or read a good book. Anything to take your mind off that... experience... and try to relax."

Kristi had obeyed. She'd curled up on the couch with her moggy cats and allowed their purring to comfort her. Stitches, her gray tabby female, gently kneaded Kristi's leg, while Between, the little tuxedo male, rested on her shoulder where he could bat away any wayward locks of hair. Fortunately, he always kept his claws sheathed when he played near Kristi's face.

Kristi stroked them, savoring the softness of their fur and the warmth of their purring bodies. "You two are the best," she said quietly. "Just the antidote I needed from the shock of the afternoon."

With her guard cats in place, Kristi drifted off for a much needed nap. When she woke, about an hour later, Stitches and Between were still purring away. Her cats took guard duty very seriously.

While she didn't feel exactly refreshed, Kristi did feel more centered after her nap. Checking the time, she decided to check the refrigerator and see what she could pull together for an evening meal. Jason would appreciate a home-cooked dinner after the day she was sure he'd endured. She didn't often have time to cook— one of the drawbacks of being a working woman — but with an unexpected afternoon off she might as well spend a little time in the kitchen.

"Come on, kitty-kids," she said as she eased out from under the cats and stood. "Let's go see what we can whip up for dinner."

Standing in front of the open refrigerator, she surveyed the contents. "Let's see," she said aloud. "Half of a rotisserie chicken. I wonder what I can do with that?" Closing her eyes, she considered. "Oh! I know! Let's see... yep, I've got a tube of biscuit dough." Grabbing the chicken and the tube of biscuits, she placed them on the counter before opening the freezer.

"Win!" Finding what she was looking for, she grabbed a bag of frozen mixed vegetables and deposited them on the counter beside the chicken. "Chicken and biscuit bake it is."

When Jason walked in the front door an hour later, he was greeted with the comforting smell of chicken simmering in a creamy sauce.

He stopped dead in his tracks and stared at Kristi. "You cooked!"

She laughed. "You don't have to sound so surprised," she teased. "I do know how."

His cheeks reddened as he pulled off his Stetson and placed it on the coat rack by the front door. "I know," he said. "It's just that you don't usually have time."

"Well, I did today." She stepped to his side and waited while he took off his sheepskin coat and hung it beside his hat. Then she put her arms around his waist and hugged him tightly. "Ruby sent me home after she heard about the carousel."

Jason stroked her back and kissed the top of her head. "Good for her. Did being home help?"

She nodded, her cheek rubbing against his khaki uniform shirt. "It did. I took a nap and then decided making dinner would keep me from brooding. The cats helped."

He laughed. She felt the comforting rumble through her face pressed against his chest. "I'm sure they did."

Kristi broke the hug and stepped away from him, but he caught her hand and intertwined their fingers. Smiling, she led him to the kitchen.

"By the way," he said, "whatever you made, it smells great."

"Chicken and biscuits," she told him. "Nice, warm comfort food." Releasing his hand, she pulled an oven mitt from a drawer and opened the oven. The smell intensified, and Jason groaned with anticipation as she pulled the casserole dish out and placed it on a hot pad.

Creamy white sauce bubbled around the edges of perfectly browned biscuits while bits of carrots, green beans, and chicken peeked from beneath the dough.

"That looks delicious," Jason said, leaning over and waving the fragrant steam toward his nose.

Kristi grinned and motioned toward the kitchen door. "Go wash up while I dish up our plates. Meet you at the table."

"You don't have to tell me twice," he said and strode from the kitchen.

The cats picked that moment to remind Kristi of their existence by winding around her ankles and meowing loudly.

She laughed. "Don't worry, kitty-kids. I haven't forgotten your dinner." As she talked to them, she filled their bowls with kibble, then opened the refrigerator and pulled out a small dish. "I even saved some bites of chicken for you. Enjoy."

With the cats fed, she plated the chicken and biscuit casserole and added a small side salad to each plate. She was just placing the plates on the table when Jason returned.

"I'll get the drinks," he said, returning a moment later with two cold colas and glasses of ice to pour them over.

Kristi nodded. "Perfect."

They made short work of their meals. Kristi was pleased with her efforts... and Jason's evident enjoyment of the food. The cream sauce was just right. Perfectly blended with just the right amount of salt and pepper. The chicken tender, and the vegetables well-cooked without being mushy. All together a good effort at a home-cooked meal.

She paused as she was about to lift a forkful of salad greens to her mouth, a small frown between her eyes.

Jason glanced up, put his fork down, and asked, "What?"

"I just realized, I never asked who that poor man was. You found out, didn't you?"

He nodded, picked up his fork and continued eating. After chewing and swallowing, he said, "We did. His name was Ray Carrick. I notified his wife this afternoon."

Kristi gasped. "Not Denise Carrick!"

Jason froze, his fork halfway to his mouth. He stared at Kristi, placed his loaded fork on his plate, and wiped his mouth on his napkin. "You know her? I thought you said you didn't recognize the victim."

She shook her head. "I didn't. I've never met him, but I know Denise. She's a quilter. She shops with us often." She paused and lowered her eyes, staring unseeing at her plate. "Oh, poor Denise. Ruby and Mattie and I will have to think of something we can do for her."

Jason reached across the table and took her hand. "I'm so sorry." He paused looked away and sighed. "I wish this death had no connection to you, but since it does, promise me you'll be careful."

She squeezed his hand and gave him a wan smile. "You talk like I run around looking for trouble." Before he could respond, she said, "Don't worry. I can't imagine that I'll be involved in any way. It's your investigation."

He picked up his fork to continue his meal, but paused to say, "Good. Just make sure that you tell me if anything occurs to you. I don't want to lose you, Kristi. Not now. Not ever."

Her heart swelled until she thought it might burst right out of her chest. He loved her! And she loved him. And they were getting married in a week!

Life was good. She was just sorry everything had fallen apart for Denise.

8

SUNDAY MORNING

Sunday. Typically Jason's staff had the day off. Only one deputy would be on duty, manning the phones and ready to call others in as needed. But this wasn't a typical Sunday. Kristi and Jason had discovered a body yesterday. He had work to do, and so did his staff.

Accordingly, Jason rose early, dressed in his uniform of khaki shirt and blue jeans, kissed Kristi's hair, and headed to the office. He stopped by *Roasted Beans* for a large cup of black coffee and a bear claw pastry and ate breakfast on the run.

As he stepped into the white stucco building that housed his department, he was pleased to see that his second-in-command, Janet Millson was already present and updating the murder board at the back of the work area.

She turned as the bell over the door chimed. "Morning, Sheriff."

Jason nodded. "Morning, Janet." He glanced at the board. Removing his sheepskin coat and throwing it on a chair, he strode closer. "Anything new?"

"The coroner's report is in." She handed him a sheaf of papers.

He flipped through the contents and nodded. "Sean says the time of death was approximately 6:00 a.m." He glanced up and said, "That's about what we expected."

"Take a look at the cause," Janet said.

Jason returned his attention to the report. "Huh. Two wounds, from two different knives, very likely delivered by two different assailants." He frowned. "Well that's definitely not what I expected."

Janet nodded. "Sounds like the one to the belly was first, but the one to the chest killed him."

Jason continued reading, his frown deepening. "But the belly wound alone would've been fatal eventually. Just not as fast as the chest wound, which nicked his heart muscle."

"Someone really wanted the man dead."

Jason grunted his agreement. "Two someones since both wounds were potentially fatal." Placing the coroner's report on the table, he studied the murder board. "Too bad the canvass of the neighborhood didn't turn up any witnesses."

"True," she agreed. "Though not surprising. Not a lot of people are out in the area surrounding the park that early in the morning."

He nodded. "And no indication that the murder took place elsewhere and the body was simply dumped at the carousel?"

"Nope. No blood trail anywhere around the carousel. Plus, the blood spatter on the carousel itself was consistent with him being knifed there." She paused and studied the pictures of the body. "Though it's possible he was standing and fell back onto the bench."

Jason picked up the coroner's report again, searched the text, and nodded. "Sean seems to think the angle of entry on the belly wound suggests the victim was standing, but that the angle on the chest wound could indicate a downward motion. Like this." He replaced the papers and acted out his thought using one of the desk chairs as his victim. "As if the victim was sitting, and the perp was standing over him."

Janet nodded. "I can see that, and it fits with Sean's statement that the belly strike was first and the chest second."

"What about the timing?" Jason asked. "Were the wounds delivered in close succession, or was there a significant delay between them?"

This time it was Janet who grabbed the report and flipped through the pages. She frowned. "Sean doesn't say." She glanced up at Jason. "Do you want me to call and find out?"

"Do that," Jason said with a nod. "I mean, if there was a delay, we might only be dealing with one assailant. He stabbed him elsewhere, then followed him and delivered the chest strike at the carousel."

"Possibly," Janet said, frowning. "But that doesn't sit well with us not finding any blood evidence in the grass around the carousel." She glanced back at the report in her hand. "Plus, Sean states that the two wounds were made by different blades."

Jason sighed. "You're right. But it sure would be easier to find one perp instead of two."

"Aren't you the one who said police work isn't meant to be easy?"

He laughed. "Caught by my own words."

The front door opened and Eric Lawson, Evan Knott, and Roger Jepperson entered the station.

"All right," Jason said. "You get in touch with Sean about the timing and then help Evan do a deep background search on Carrick. Find out who his enemies are... all the way back to childhood if necessary." He shrugged into his coat and motioned for Eric to keep his on. "I'll take Eric with me to interview Carrick's employer and his younger brother. Roger, head home. I'll need you to come in this evening to be on call."

Janet nodded. "Sounds like a plan."

Roger turned around, calling, "Yes, sir," over his shoulder.

"Eric," Jason said, "grab the contact information for Franz Kecskés and Davey Carrick. We'll check Kecskés Auto Repair first, but if Franz isn't there, I'll need you to do some phone work while I drive."

"Yes, sir," Deputy Lawson replied as he stopped by the table and found the data the sheriff had requested. Once he'd copied what he needed into his notebook, he glanced at his boss. "Ready, sir."

Jason nodded. "Then let's roll."

As they walked to his vehicle, Jason said, "Call Davey Carrick. See if you can set up a time to meet him. Once that's done, call Mark Robards and ask him to meet us there."

"Sorry, sir, but I don't have Robards' number."

"I do." Jason opened his cell phone and read the number off while Lawson added it to his notebook.

A few minutes later, Jason pulled his Trail Blazer to a stop in front of the repair shop. The business was closed, it being Sunday, but a light shone through a window to the side of the working area of the shop.

"Looks like Mr. Kecskés might be here," Jason said, reaching for his door handle. "Let's go find out." The two lawmen stepped out of the vehicle and walked to the shop's front door.

Knocking loudly, Jason called, "Mr. Kecskés! It's Sheriff Reynolds. I need to speak with you."

A few moments later the door was opened by a grizzled-looking man. Salt and pepper hair, blue-gray eyes, cheeks covered with a bristle of graying stubble, and a prominent nose that looked like it had been broken more than once. He was solidly built, with an almost nonexistent neck. Maybe 5'8" in height.

"I'm Franz Kecskés," the man said, eyeing Jason and then Lawson. "What can I do for you, Sheriff."

"Is there somewhere we can talk, Mr. Kecskés?" Jason asked. "I'd rather not discuss this on your doorstep."

Kecskés grunted, beckoned them inside, and led them through the repair bay to a small, dingy office. The walls had once been white, but had grayed with age, much like their owner. A beat up desk was covered in papers, with an ancient computer sitting precariously to one side.

Kecskés moved to the back of the desk and seated himself in a creaky rolling chair. He motioned Jason into the single folding chair that sat across from him. Deputy Lawson found a spot to lean against the wall.

"So, what brings you to my shop on a Sunday, Sheriff?"

Jason inhaled deeply and asked, "Do you employ a man named Ray Carrick?"

Kecskés' eyes narrowed. "I do. Has he done something wrong?"

Jason shook his head. "I'm sorry to inform you that Mr. Carrick is dead. His body was found in Riverside Park yesterday afternoon."

"Dead?" Kecskés' straightened his back, his eyes widening. "How can he be dead? He's only in his thirties." He drew a deep breath, then asked more quietly, "How did he die?"

"He was murdered." Jason waited a beat for that statement to sink in, then asked, "Do you know anyone who had reason to wish him dead?"

Kecskés shook his head, his face paling. "No. I don't." He paused, licked his lips, and then continued, "Ray was a hard worker. Knew his way around an engine. Any engine, actually. One of the best mechanics I've ever employed. The customers liked him. He was quiet, but always pleasant. Some even asked for him by name."

He scrubbed a hand across his face, then met Jason's gaze. "No. I can't think of anyone who disliked him, let alone hated him enough to murder him." He paused, then asked, "Are you sure it was murder? Not just some freak accident?"

Jason studied the man. "We're sure." He stood and held out his hand to Kecskés. "Thank you for your time, Mr. Kecskés. If you think of anything that might be of help, please call."

He paused as Kecskés rose and shook his extended hand. "And, I'm very sorry for your loss."

Once they were back in the Trail Blazer, Jason turned to his deputy. "What do you think?"

Eric met his gaze. "He sure seemed genuine. Seemed to like the victim."

Jason nodded and started the engine. "My thoughts exactly, but we'll keep an open mind. Now, what time are we meeting Davey and Mark? And where?"

"Mark will be at Davey Carrick's place in about ten minutes. He said he'd keep Davey calm until we got there, since I wasn't sure how long we'd need with Mr. Kecskés."

"Great work, Eric. Give me the address."

9

SUNDAY NOON

After a busy morning of housecleaning, Kristi settled down at her scrubbed oak breakfast table to eat her lunch and enjoy the view from the picture window beside the table. This view of the majestic Absaroka mountain range had been one of the reasons she'd chosen to purchase this house. She'd always loved the 'Sorkees, and being able to enjoy the view while she ate always relaxed her.

And she needed relaxation and peace today.

She'd worked hard all morning, partly to be ready for her parents arrival on Tuesday— they'd be staying with her, and she wanted the guest bedroom to be spotless!— but more to keep herself from thinking about the body she'd found yesterday. But now that she was sitting still and supposedly enjoying a garden salad topped with bits of chopped rotisserie chicken and creamy ranch dressing, her thoughts kept trying to return to that poor man.

To combat the visions of his lifeless body, she alternately stared out the window at the 'Sorkees or chatted with her cats, Stitches and Between. Her kitty-kids perched on the padded bench beneath the window watching every forkful of salad hoping Kristi might drop a bite of chicken.

After taking a sip of tea to clear her throat, Kristi glanced at her cats and relented. "Fine. You can each have one bite of chicken." She picked out two little bits not too covered in dressing and presented them, one to each cat.

Stitches took hers delicately, being careful not to touch Kristi's fingers. Between lunged forward and attacked the offered bite as though it might try to escape.

Kristi laughed, wiped her fingers on her napkin, and scooped the final bit of her salad into her mouth. She was carrying her dishes to the sink, accompanied by both cats— just in case!— when her cell phone rang. Glancing at the readout, she was pleased to see Stacy's name.

Awesome! Another diversion.

Accepting the call, she moved to the living room as she spoke. "Hey, Stacy. What's up?"

"I have news," Stacy said, her voice vibrating with excitement. "Are you sitting down?"

Kristi settled in the corner of her forest green couch and grinned. "I am now. What's got you so excited?"

"I found your venue and booked it," Stacy said with a little squeal. "It's going to be perfect!"

Kristi's heart hammered. Would Stacy's idea of *perfect* match hers? Or Jason's? With a bit of trepidation in her heart, she said, "Don't keep me in suspense! Where is it?"

"The Garnet Gateway Inn! They have a lovely conference room on the second floor that's a perfect size for a small wedding, and it even has arched windows at one end that look out at the

Absarokas! What an awesome backdrop for you and Jason as you take your vows, don't you think?"

Kristi's breath caught. A view of the 'Sorkees as she and Jason exchanged vows! What could be more perfect? "Oh, Stacy! That sounds amazing. And the room is available this Saturday?" She couldn't believe they could get such a wonderful venue on such short notice. She held her breath as she waited for Stacy's response.

"Sure is," Stacy said with a giggle. "I snapped it up at once. You and Jason are getting married at the Garnet Gateway Inn!"

Fear suddenly niggled at Kristi's good mood. This was too good to be true. There had to be a catch. "How much will this cost, Stacy?"

"Oh!" Stacy said in a breathless voice. "That's one of the best parts. Since it wasn't already booked, and it was too last minute to reasonably expect to rent it out, and since it was me asking— I *am* the premier real estate agent in the area and bring them a lot of customers, you know, out-of-towners here scouting out property— they're giving us a deep discount." She paused for breath. "It's easily within the budget we discussed."

Kristi breathed a sigh of relief. "Stacy, that is awesome news. Thank you so much. I never would've even considered the Inn. I'd have assumed it was too expensive and too unavailable at such a late date."

"Yep," Stacy agreed. "I'm amazing!"

Both women laughed.

"And," Stacy continued, "If you'd like, they'll even provide your wedding cake and a "Farewell Champagne Brunch" so your guests can celebrate as you leave for your honeymoon. And before you ask, the price they quoted me was very reasonable."

"Wow! A wedding and reception all in one place. How cool is that?"

She could almost see Stacy nodding. "I thought you'd be pleased."

"Now all I have to do is get the invitations out," Kristi said. "Couldn't do that until I had a venue."

"Do you need help?"

Kristi shook her head, though Stacy couldn't see her. "No. Jason and I are going to do that together. I'm writing, he's addressing."

"Good plan. I'll look forward to getting mine!"

They spent a few more minutes discussing brunch menus and prices before agreeing that Stacy should finalize the arrangements with the Inn. Wedding at 3:00 p.m., followed by the reception with a champagne brunch and a mix of petit fours decorated in fall colors in lieu of a wedding cake.

After ending the call, Kristi turned to Stitches and Between who were lounging on the back of the couch. "It's really happening! Jason and I are getting married next Saturday and we're going to have a real wedding… not just a few friends here in the living room." She shook her head as she reached to stroke first one cat, then the other. "I can't believe it." She took a deep breath as her eyes teared up. "Friends really are amazing. Mine are making this wedding more beautiful than I thought possible."

SUNDAY AFTERNOON

When Jason parked his Trail Blazer across the street from Davey Carrick's place, he was pleased to see that Mark Robards' Chevy pickup was already in the drive. Turning to his deputy, Eric Lawson, Jason said, "Looks like Mark beat us here." He reached for the door handle and pulled. "Let's get this done."

The two lawmen strode across the street and up to the front door. Jason knocked. The door opened promptly to reveal Mark Robards.

"Sheriff Reynolds," Mark said. "Deputy Lawson. Step inside. Davey is ready for you."

Jason nodded and stepped in, removing his Stetson as he did so. Glancing around he noted a compact living space, white walls in need of a paint job, and well-worn furniture including a nondescript brown couch and a couple of mismatched chairs. Davey Carrick stood beside a beat up book shelf that was overflowing with paperbacks and magazines.

The man was a reader. That surprised Jason, though it shouldn't have. He tried not to classify folks before he knew them. A productive investigation required an open mind. He took a deep breath and stepped toward the victim's brother.

"Thank you for seeing us, Mr. Carrick. We're very sorry for your loss."

Davey Carrick closed his eyes for a moment. When he opened them, he looked pained.

"Appreciate that, Sheriff. Please, have a seat."

Davey and Mark seated themselves on the old couch, leaving Jason and Eric to take the mismatched chairs. The two lawmen opened their shearling coats and sat, placing their Stetsons on the floor beside their feet.

When everyone was seated, Davey asked, "How can I help?"

"We'd like to get a feel for your brother's life. We know he was an auto mechanic and was married, but what can you tell us about him?"

Davey leaned forward, elbows on knees, and gazed at the worn beige carpet beneath his feet. A few moments passed before he spoke.

"Ray was a good man. A good brother. Sure, we had our moments. I think Mom worried that one of us would kill the other before we made it to adulthood, but it was really just kid stuff. Boys trying to one up each other. We finally outgrew it. Especially after he married Denise. She was good for him and he loved her deeply."

He paused and looked up, meeting Jason's eyes, his face etched with pain. "We didn't see each other as often as we should've, especially after Mom and Dad retired and moved to Billings. The family got together at Christmas, but other than that I didn't see much of Ray and Denise.

"Well, Ray would call me once or twice each summer to see if I wanted to go fly fishing, but that was all." He glanced at Mark. "Summer's our busiest time for construction, so we didn't manage to fish more than a couple of times each year."

Mark laid a hand on Davey's shoulder. "Davey rarely asks for a day off, so I try to accommodate him when I can." He squeezed the young man's shoulder, then dropped his hand to his lap. "Davey's a good worker. I'm lucky to have him on my team."

Jason nodded. "Did Ray have any other hobbies, other than fly fishing?"

"He liked to carve." Davey stood and walked to the bookshelf where he lifted a pile of magazines and extracted a small figurine. Carrying it back to the couch, he handed it to Jason. "He wasn't very good at it, but he said it relaxed him." He aimed a sad smile at Jason. "That's supposed to be a bear. I could never figure out which part was the head."

Jason handed the little carving, which looked more like a blob than a bear, to Eric who returned it to the shelf after turning it over in his hands a few times.

Taking a deep breath, Jason steeled himself and looked Davey directly in the eyes. "I'm sorry, Mr. Carrick, but was your brother into anything dangerous? Drugs? Illicit firearms? Gang activity?"

Davey's face paled. "Ray? Do something illegal? No! Absolutely not." He stood and paced across the room and back, stopping behind the couch, across from Jason. "No. If anything, he'd've gotten in trouble by trying to keep someone else from crossing a line."

Jason pounced. "Who, Davey? Who were his friends? Who would he have tried to keep safe and on the right side of the law?"

Davey leaned forward, hands braced on the back of the couch. He glared at Jason for a moment, then seemed to wilt. Straightening, he stepped around the end of the couch and resumed his seat beside Mark.

"Okay. He had some friends from high school. Guys that were always looking for a fast buck, an easy score. They skirted the law, but were never charged with anything." He took a deep breath, let it out, then continued earnestly, "But they moved up to Helena about the time Ray and Denise got married. Denise didn't like them. Thought they were trouble, so Ray was ready to cut ties even before they moved. I haven't seen any of them in years."

Jason nodded and pulled out his notebook. Eric did the same.

"Names?" Jason asked.

Davey frowned, but answered promptly. "Billy Jennings, Tommie Atwood, and Steve Gibbs."

Jason wrote the names in his little notebook, pausing over that last one as a thought niggled at his brain. Gibbs. Why did that sound familiar? Then it hit him.

"Steve Gibbs. Any relation to Eula Gibbs?" The older woman who worked part-time for Kristi and sold baby quilts on consignment in Kristi's shop.

Davey nodded. "I think that's Steve's grandmother's name." After a moment, he exclaimed, "Oh! And there was Jerry Wanamaker." His face fell. "But he's been dead for a few years."

"Huh," Jason said. "What happened to him?"

"He ODed." Davey frowned. "Weird though. His body was found on the carousel too."

A tingle ran down Jason's spine. The carousel again. But why didn't he remember a body being found there before Ray

Carrick's? He grabbed his Stetson and stood. "You've been a big help, Mr. Carrick. If you think of anything else, anything at all, give us a call." He nodded to Mark. "Thanks for your help, Mark. Appreciate it."

The other three men rose. Mark nodded. "I didn't really do anything, but I'm glad to help."

Davey bumped Mark's shoulder. "Actually, you did. It was a lot easier to think with a friendly face in the room." He paused, his face reddening. "Not that you're unfriendly, Sheriff... or you, Deputy."

Jason smiled. "Don't worry about it, Mr. Carrick. That's why I asked Mark to join us."

They moved to the front door, where Jason paused with his hand on the door knob. "Again, Mr. Carrick, we're sorry for your loss and appreciate you taking the time to answer our questions."

Davey nodded. "If I think of anything, I'll let you know."

Jason and Eric strode across the street without a word. Once they were inside the Trail Blazer, Jason turned to Eric, "Do you know anything about the Wanamaker death?"

Eric shook his head. "No sir. But if it was a few years ago, it may have been before I joined the department."

Jason blew out a breath. "I'll check with Janet. If she doesn't remember, we'll go through the files until we find it."

"You think it's related?"

"Probably not, but it's a connection to be checked out." Jason turned the key in the ignition and the Trail Blazer roared to life. "By the way, nice job in there. Appreciated you staying quiet and just observing. What did you think?"

Eric's cheeks reddened at the compliment. "Well, if he's into anything shady, he's not making any money. Everything in there needs to be replaced and upgraded."

"True. Plus, Mark's a good friend. I trust his assessment of the man. What else?"

"Whether it's true or not, he believes his brother was an upstanding citizen and not involved in any criminal activity. But those names he gave us. Those could be a solid lead, not to mention the dead guy."

Jason nodded, checked for traffic, and pulled away from the curb. "Agreed. When we get back to the station, I want you to start background checks on all three men. Find out where they are now and if any of them have been back to Garnet Gateway recently. Have Roger take over at shift change. I'll see what I can find out about the dead guy on the carousel."

Eric jotted a note in his notebook. "Will do, Sheriff."

SUNDAY EVENING

By dinner time, Kristi was exhausted. She'd cleaned the entire house, even vacuuming the walls and washing the ceiling fixtures, and the only break had been lunch and a conversation with Stacy. She definitely wasn't up for cooking a meal.

She called Jason, who was usually off duty on the weekend, to find out what time he expected to be home. Once she had a time frame, she called Rizzoli's, placed a take-out order, and at the appropriate time dragged herself to the car to go pick up their food.

When Jason walked in the front door, Kristi was just plating their dinner. She'd ordered spaghetti and meatballs for Jason, his favorite, and lasagna for herself. Rizzoli's always provided a full meal, including generous side salads and fresh focaccia bread. The only thing missing from their usual restaurant dinner was a bottle of chianti, but she knew Jason would be fine with a beer and she'd enjoy a coke.

Jason removed his shearling coat and his Stetson and parked them on the coat rack near the front door. "Wow! Something smells fabulous." He took a moment to scan the living area, and then asked, "How did you find time to cook today? I can tell you've been busy; the house fairly shines."

"Thank you, and I didn't," she said with a laugh. "We're having take out from Rizzoli's."

He nodded and moved to help her get everything to the table. "Great choice. Their food is always delicious."

Once everything was in place, they took their seats at the dining table. Jason smiled happily and said, "I love their spaghetti and meatballs," before digging into his meal.

Kristi grinned. "Don't I know it. You order it every time we eat there." When she scooped a forkful of lasagna into her mouth, she almost groaned with relief. Food! Really *good* food after an exhausting day of preparing for her parents' arrival. What could be better? Nothing, she decided, and she closed her eyes to better enjoy the perfectly spiced beef, rich tomato sauce, and gooey cheese. Rizzoli's turned baking lasagna into an art form!

As always, Jason finished his meal first, leaning back in his chair and sipping his beer. "That was delicious." While he waited for Kristi to finish, he told her about his day. Not the details of the investigation, just a rough outline of where he'd been and who he'd seen.

Swallowing the last bite of focaccia bread soaked in the final remains of her red sauce, Kristi leaned back, too full to contemplate clearing the table... or even moving!

"I'm glad Mark was able to help you interview Davey," she said after wiping her lips with her napkin. "I can't imagine how hard it must've been to answer questions when he's grieving the loss of his brother."

Jason nodded. "I think Mark's presence helped Davey stay calm."

"Was he able to help you at all?"

"As a matter of fact, he provided some names that we'll be checking into tomorrow."

"That's good." She stood, stretched, and picked up her plate. Jason followed suit and between the two of them, they soon had the table cleared, the dishwasher loaded, and the few leftovers refrigerated.

As they meandered toward the living room, Kristi said, "Oh! I forgot to tell you. Stacy called earlier. We have a venue! We're getting married at the Garnet Gateway Inn!"

Jason settled on the couch and pulled her down next to him. "I'm guessing this is a good thing since you sound excited."

"It is," she said, nearly bouncing on the seat cushion. "Stacy told me all about it. The room sounds perfect— it even has a view of the 'Sorkees!— and the Inn will provide a reception buffet and petit fours for our wedding cake." She stopped to take a breath, gave him a bright smile, and then added, "And maybe the best part is the price. They gave Stacy a screaming deal because, one: it's last minute and they had no hope of renting the room otherwise, and two: it was Stacy asking and she sends them a *lot* of business."

"Sounds like Stacy really came through for us."

Kristi beamed at him. "She did, and the whole deal is well within our budget."

He pulled her into his arms and kissed her soundly. When they broke apart, he held her away from him and grinned. "It's all coming together, isn't it?"

She grinned back and then snuggled against his side. "It is. We're getting married in less than a week… and it's going to be a beautiful ceremony!"

They relaxed in comfortable silence for a few minutes before Kristi stirred.

"This is wonderful, but if I sit still much longer I'll be in danger of falling asleep. It's been a busy day."

"And what's wrong with that?" Jason asked, smoothing her hair away from her face.

"Not a thing, except I have wedding invitations to write and they really should go out first thing tomorrow since we're getting married on Saturday and Thursday is a holiday."

Jason sighed. "You're right, and now that we know the venue, there's no excuse not to get that little chore done." He moved her gently aside and prepared to stand, but stopped and looked at her. "Do you have the card stock you want to use?"

"Yes, and I've already drafted the text. I was just waiting for the venue."

"Dining table?" he asked.

She nodded. "That'll give us plenty of room."

"You write and I'll address. Where did we put the list?"

She stood and walked to a small desk in the corner. "Right here, but you'd be better off with my laptop. I have a spreadsheet with names and addresses."

"Perfect."

They gathered what they needed to get the job done and set to work. When all twenty invitations were addressed, sealed, and stamped, they gave each other a weary thumbs up.

"Time for bed," Kristi said with a jaw-cracking yawn.

Jason nodded, and eyeing his soon-to-be wife, added, "Time for *sleep*. We'll content ourselves with snuggling tonight."

"Saving up for the honeymoon?" Kristi teased.

"Just saving my exhausted almost-wife," Jason said, putting an arm around her shoulders and steering her toward the bedroom where Stitches and Between sprawled across the king-size quilt. Jason rolled his eyes, then glared at the cats.

"Make yourselves scarce, kitty-kids" he said. "Your mom needs her rest."

Stitches stood, stretched, then marched to the edge of the bed and hopped down. Between followed her lead, but with his tail held high. Just to make sure Jason understood he was doing this because he wanted to, not because a mere mortal had commanded him.

Kristi giggled. "I'm not sure how you do that."

Jason nodded her toward the bathroom. "It's a sheriff thing. Now get your PJs on!"

MONDAY MORNING

Deputy Roger Jepperson was shrugging into his coat when Sheriff Jason Reynolds strode into the station Monday morning.

"Any developments overnight, Roger?"

"No, sir. I finished what I could on the background checks you asked for. Left my findings on Eric's desk so he can check in with the sources that weren't available over the weekend."

Jason nodded. "Good enough. You're off duty until tomorrow. I've arranged for Evan to take the late shift tonight."

Roger gave him a tired smile. "Thanks, Sheriff. Call if you need me sooner."

"You know I will. Now go get some shut eye."

Jason continued to his office, nodding as he heard the rest of his staff arriving for the day shift. Closing the door, he removed his coat and hat, hanging them on the coat rack before seating himself behind his desk. Reaching for the stack of papers in his inbox, he read through the information they'd gathered so far.

Sean's coroner's report indicated that the victim had died at around 6 a.m.; that the two stab wounds had been delivered by two different weapons; and that though either would have proved fatal, the chest wound was the official cause of death.

Jason shook his head. What had an engine mechanic gotten himself into that would cause *two* assailants to want him dead?

Dropping Sean's report on his desk, Jason picked up Janet's findings on Ray Carrick. After a thorough reading, he dropped the papers and turned to stare out the window. The victim's background provided no clues. His finances were in order. The man wasn't rich, but he and his wife lived within their means with no unexplained deposits or withdrawals and no unusual accounts or safety deposit boxes that his deputies had been able to unearth. He was a good mechanic and seemed to be well-liked. In short, he was a good man. A reliable man. Just the kind of clean-cut, hard-working citizen Garnet Gateway liked to boast about.

But somebody hadn't liked him. *Two* somebodies had disliked him strongly enough to knife him to death.

A knock sounded on his door. Jason swiveled back to face his desk and called, "Come."

Janet Millson, his second-in-command, opened the door and stepped inside.

"Finally managed to connect with the coroner," she said. "The timing on when the wounds were inflicted will depend on the results of the bloodwork and histological tests. He doesn't expect to have those until tomorrow at the earliest. Possibly not until the end of the week."

Jason sighed, but nodded. "Okay. Thanks for following up, Janet."

She stepped closer to his desk. "I saw that Eric added some names to the murder board. Viable suspects?"

Jason motioned for her to sit, which she did. "More like persons of interest," he said. "Friends from Carrick's high school days. Trouble makers. Guys his wife was happy to see leave the area. Eric and Roger started background searches. Eric should be able to finish those up now that it's Monday and regular business hours have resumed."

She stared past him, through the window behind his desk. After a moment, she met his gaze. "Any hunches so far?"

He picked up her background report, flipped through it, and dropped it back on his desk. "With a citizen as solid as Carrick appears to be, I'm guessing he saw something he shouldn't have and the perps had to take him out before he could report what he'd seen. Wrong place, wrong time."

Janet nodded. "And the old friends?"

"They moved away a few years ago, so they may not figure into this, but..."

"But if any of them happened to be in town this weekend, we could have a solid lead."

Jason tapped his fingers on the desk. "And Thanksgiving is coming up. Any or all of them could be home for the holiday and Ray could've agreed to meet one of them on the sly... given his wife wasn't a fan. The question is, what could they be up to in Garnet Gateway that would be worth murdering an old friend over?"

"We're not exactly a hotbed of crime," Janet agreed with a shoulder shrug, "but that doesn't mean some enterprising soul wouldn't be willing to try to bring drugs or prostitution here."

"True. This could even be a hunting ground for human trafficking." Jason closed his eyes for a moment. "We've got a lot of healthy, outdoor types who'd bring a good profit. Of course, we're also a close-knit community who would notice the loss of our daughters or sons."

"Agreed. Which is why I lean towards drugs." She shook her head. "No place is safe from the drug trade."

"Speaking of drugs, do you remember a man named Jerry Wanamaker? Davey Carrick also mentioned his name, but said he'd died of a drug overdose a few years ago. That his body was found on the carousel. Thing is, I don't remember that case."

Janet frowned for a moment before her face cleared and she nodded. "Yep. I remember. It happened over that long weekend when you went to Denver for that convention. You weren't here, so you weren't involved. I'm sure you read my report once you were back in the office."

Jason winced. Of course he remembered that weekend, that convention. That was when he'd made the supremely stupid choice to have a one-night-stand. The liaison that had ended his first marriage to Kristi. No wonder he didn't remember reading the report on Wanamaker; his personal life had been falling apart. It had taken him this long to get his relationship with Kristi, the love of his life, back on track. And here was an event from that fateful weekend cropping up again.

Before he could decide on an appropriate comment, the intercom sounded and he answered gratefully. "What is it, Clara?"

"Ray Carrick's parents are on the line for you, Sheriff."

"Thanks," he said with a sigh. "Put them through, Clara."

Janet stood. "I'll go help Eric finish up those background checks," she said as she moved to the door. "Open or closed?"

"Close it, please."

She nodded and did so as Jason picked up the phone to deal with the current victim's parents.

13

MONDAY MIDMORNING

Kristi tried not to feel panicked as she washed the breakfast dishes, fed the cats, and told Stitches and Between to be good before grabbing her coat and her embroidered denim shoulder bag and racing out of the house. So many things to do today! But first and foremost, she had to mail the invitations to her wedding.

Patting her bag to make sure the invitations were still where she'd put them the night before, she smiled. Her wedding! She and Jason were actually doing it. This time next week she'd be Mrs. Reynolds. Again.

With a laugh, she realized the *again* part no longer stung. Jason had made a mistake— and they'd both paid for it— but he'd also put in the time and work to reestablish trust. They were marrying again, and they'd be stronger for the time they'd spent apart. They'd gained a deep realization that they were each what the other wanted, more than anything else.

Their love was true, and while that didn't mean they'd have a fairy tale existence, it did mean they'd trust each other enough to work through whatever came their way. After all, this was their story and they'd write their way.

But today... today was likely to be hectic.

She ticked off her to-do list in her head as she drove into town. First stop: post office. Mail those invitations! Next stop: *Delectable Mountain Quilting*. Today was her last day in her quilt shop until after the honeymoon. (The honeymoon!!) Finally: *Delilah's Dresses!* She had a date with Mattie and Ruby this evening to shop for her wedding dress. God! She hoped Delilah would have something appropriate. She wanted to look her best, but she didn't want a fancy white gown. She'd done that once. Never again.

She pulled her bright red Subaru Outback into the post office and glanced longingly at the official drop box. It would only take a minute to pull through the lane and drop her invitations into the slot. BUT... she'd feel more secure if she handed them directly to Garnet Gateway's postmaster. After all, the wedding would take place on Saturday and it was already Monday. They were cutting it close enough without adding lost invitations to the mix.

Chiding herself for being a worrywart, she nonetheless parked and walked into the post office. Garnet Gateway's post office was a small building consisting of a main room lined on three sides with rental boxes for those who didn't have—or preferred not to have—mail delivered to their home. The fourth side was taken up by a sales counter, where a postal worker accepted mail, sold stamps, and weighed and assessed parcels. The worker on duty this morning was Eva Brandt, a fairly regular customer of Kristi's.

Eva looked up and smiled as Kristi approached the counter. "Good morning, Kristi. How can I help?"

"Good morning to you, too, Eva." Kristi pulled her stack of addressed, stamped, and sealed invitations out of her denim shoulder bag and laid them on the counter. "I just need to mail these. Didn't feel like dropping them in the box."

Eva laughed. "You'd be surprised how many folks prefer putting their mail directly into human hands." She scooped up the invitations and dropped them in a mail bin at her side. "Not to worry. These will go out in this morning's mail."

Turning to leave, Kristi grinned and said over her shoulder, "Thanks, Eva. Have a great day!"

Once in her Subaru, Kristi backed out of the parking space and turned onto Main Street. Invitations safely mailed. Check. Next stop: *Delectable Mountain Quilting*. After parking in the small, gravel lot behind the shop, Kristi sat still for a moment and allowed her nerves to settle. Suddenly, everything seemed to be moving too fast. She'd bought this quilt shop from Mattie Stebbings just over a year and a half ago. Stacy Akins had been her real estate agent, and Mark Robards had done the remodel. Now the two of them were married… and were about to stand up for her own marriage to Jason.

A year and a half… and her life was about to change again. She shook her head, reminding herself that the last change had really started a little over two and a half years ago when she and Jason had divorced. Their marriage had lost two and a half years. Still, it had ended well. If they hadn't divorced, she probably wouldn't have stepped out on her own to buy the shop, and Kristi loved owning *Delectable Mountain Quilting*. Plus, she really believed she and Jason were in a better, more stable and loving relationship now than they had been in their marriage's last incarnation.

As the saying goes, all's well that ends well.

Nodding to herself, Kristi stepped out of her Subaru and headed through the back door and into her quilt shop. She had a lot of work to do today. Schedules to finalize, inventory to check, and customers to greet. Life was good!

After pausing in the kitchen / break room to put her down jacket and denim shoulder bag in her locker, Kristi moved into the main part of her store. Noticing activity in the classroom, she paused at the door to peer in. No classes were scheduled for this week, what with Thanksgiving on Thursday. Who was doing what?

Mattie and Ruby looked up from the large quilt frame that sat in the middle of the room. Mattie sprang to her feet and rushed to Kristi's side where she took her arm and firmly guided her away from the classroom.

"Oh no you don't," she said decisively. "You're not seeing that quilt until after your honeymoon when we've placed it lovingly on your bed."

Kristi stared at Mattie, then glanced back over her shoulder. "Seriously? You're not going to let me see it while it's in progress?"

"Nope," Mattie said with a grin. "We all agreed. You're banned from peeking."

"But I know it's a Double Wedding Ring," Kristi practically wailed, "and I helped pick out the fabrics!"

"That you did. And now you'll just have to wait until it's finished. Now shoo. Go up front and talk to Eula."

"Fine," Kristi muttered and stomped toward the front of the shop. She calmed as she moved through the shelves of quilting cottons, trailing her fingers over bolts of fine quality cotton as smooth as silk. Her shop had a fabulous selection, from pastels to vivid, color-drenched patterns. From cute baby prints to gorgeous batiks. From tone-on-tone backing fabrics to seasonal flannels, she tried to make sure her shop had something for everyone, and that every bolt was of the highest quality. After all, quilts should be made to last.

"Morning, Eula," she said, plopping into the overstuffed chair she'd placed by the front window for use by husbands of her customers. "Were you banned from the classroom too?"

"Not hardly," the gray-haired senior said with a laugh. "Someone has to mind the store." She gave Kristi a grandmotherly smile. Standing barely five feet tall, Eula was nearly as wide as she was tall, and behind her wire-rimmed glasses her soft features fairly glowed with maternal comfort and charm. "Besides, we'll switch out soon and I'll have my turn to quilt."

Kristi huffed. "It's a conspiracy. And in my own shop!"

Eula nodded. "It is indeed, and all of us are involved. Andrea will be in later this afternoon to take a turn. Why even DeAnna is going to add a few stitches, and our bookkeeper is no quilter." She stepped to Kristi's side and patted her employer's hand. "But we all love you, Kristi, so be a good sport and don't give us any grief."

Kristi placed her free hand over Eula's. "Of course not, Eula," she said quietly. "But you know Mattie would be disappointed if I didn't put on a bit of a show."

Eula's laughter was light and breezy as she returned to her stool behind the counter. Once settled, her expression grew serious. "There's something I'd like to talk to you about, Kristi."

Kristi straightened and gave her friend her full attention. "Is there a problem, Eula? Am I asking you to work too many hours?"

Eula waved Kristi's concerns away. "Nothing like that, but I'm concerned about my grandson and I wanted to ask you whether or not I should bother the sheriff with what I overheard."

Kristi nodded. "Tell me."

Eula adjusted her glasses on her nose, glanced down at her clasped hands, then met Kristi's gaze. "Well, Steve, that's my grandson, is home for Thanksgiving. He and a couple of friends moved to Helena a few years ago. I haven't seen much of him recently, but I know he had his issues in high school."

"What kind of issues?" Kristi asked.

"To put it bluntly," Eula said with a grimace, "he was a hell-raiser. If there was trouble afoot, Steve was in the middle of it. For all I know, he could still be causing trouble, only now it's in Helena instead of here in my own back yard."

"Okay," Kristi said, nodding. "What has you concerned at the moment."

"Well, I heard about Ray Carrick. That you found the body over the weekend."

Kristi's heart raced. She hated that memory, but she kept her expression neutral. "That's right."

"Ray was one of Steve's best friends. At least, until Ray and Denise got serious. Denise didn't approve of Steve and the other boys. She thought—wisely, in my opinion—they were a bad influence.

"Anyway, yesterday afternoon I was headed to the kitchen to make a cup of tea when I passed Steve in the hallway. He was talking on his cell phone and I happened to hear him mention Ray's name."

She licked her lips, her hands clenched so tightly in her lap that her knuckles were white. "He said, 'If he went after Ray, you know we're next.'"

"Oh, Eula," Kristi murmured and stood, putting her arms around the woman. "Yes. You should definitely tell Jason about this."

Eula nodded, her body shivering in Kristi's arms.

14

MONDAY AFTERNOON

Sheriff Jason Reynolds leaned back in his desk chair, hands steepled below his chin, and stared out the window at the gray, wintry day. No snow yet, but the overcast sky told him it wouldn't be long before the blizzards began. He'd just hung up the phone from a call from Eula Gibbs. Kristi had insisted that her employee pass on the information Eula had overheard yesterday afternoon.

Jason was glad she had. If accurate, it could provide the tie between the two deaths at the carousel. The first had been ruled an accidental overdose, but if the second— the body he and Kristi had found on Saturday— was related, the initial ruling might have been in error.

He needed more information.

Standing, he left his office and joined his deputies to hear what they'd discovered and add his own bit of news. Striding to the murder board at the back of the work area, he studied the information and names they'd gathered so far. Nothing stood out yet, but a picture was coming into focus. His team was doing a good job.

"All right," he said. "What do we know about Jennings, Atwood, and Gibbs?"

His chief deputy, Janet Millson, caught Eric Lawson's eye and gave him an encouraging nod. Deputy Lawson stood and gave the sheriff a quick run-down.

"All three men currently reside in Helena, with Jennings and Atwood living in the same apartment complex. Gibbs, who has family in the city, currently lives in an apartment over his uncle's garage. All are employed in minimum wage, unskilled jobs. Jennings works as a bouncer at a local biker bar. Atwood is a stock boy for a nearby grocery store, and Gibbs is on the janitorial staff for Sisters of Mercy Hospital."

Jason nodded. "Any of them have rap sheets?"

"Atwood and Gibbs have been picked up a couple of times on suspicion of theft," Janet said, looking through a written copy of Eric's report, "but so far nothing has stuck. Jennings is under investigation for drug dealing, but he hasn't been charged… yet."

"Right," Jason said, staring at the photos of the men pinned to the murder board. "So we have three questionable characters, all of whom were connected to our victim in the past." He turned back to his deputies. "I happen to know that Gibbs is in town. Are either of the others?"

At his teams questioning looks, he explained. "I had a call from Gibbs' grandmother this morning. Eula works for Kristi."

"Okay," Janet said. "I guess you'll tell us why in good time."

Jason nodded. "The others?"

Eric straightened his shoulders and said. "They're all home for Thanksgiving. Atwood is staying with his family at the Rocking J Ranch, his father is the foreman. Jennings is here in town." His gaze met Jason's. "The Jennings family lives two blocks from Riverside Park."

"That could be significant. Add it to the board."

While Eric made the notation, Jason paced in front of the desks, thinking. When he came to a stop, he folded his arms across his chest.

"All right. Back to Eula Gibbs. She confided in Kristi that she was concerned about her grandson, Steve. When she told Kristi what had her worried, Kristi insisted she call me." He paused and met his deputies' gazes. "As you can imagine, that wasn't Eula's first instinct. A grandmother isn't anxious to bring her grandchild to the attention of the law... but concern for his safety had her asking Kristi's opinion as to whether or not it was important enough to tell me."

Janet frowned. "Sounds serious. What did she hear?"

"Steve was on the phone, and as she passed by Eula overheard him say, 'If he went after Ray, you know we're next.'"

Eric whistled softly. "That sounds ominous."

Janet nodded. "It also sounds like Gibbs knows who killed Ray Carrick."

"That it does," Jason agreed. "I think we need to have a chat with Steve Gibbs." He paused, considered, then continued, "But before we do, I'd like a little more background information." He turned back to the murder board and tapped a picture of the carousel. "There have been two deaths at this carousel and my gut tells me they're connected."

Turning back to his team he said, "Janet, dig out the files on Wanamaker and go over them with a critical eye. I want to know if there are any connections. Eric, get Wanamaker's date of death from the file. Find out where Jennings, Atwood, Gibbs... and Ray Carrick were on that date, and if any of them were in Garnet Gateway, see if you can figure out where they might have been and what they might have been up to."

Janet narrowed her eyes as she studied the board. "I'll take care of it, sheriff."

Eric nodded and said, "Yes, sir."

"We'll plan to interview Gibbs and the others in the morning," Jason said. His cell rang. Glancing at the display, he saw that it was Kristi. Smiling, he answered as he strode back to his office and closed the door.

"What can I do for you, Kristi?"

"Not a thing, Sheriff Reynolds," she said, and Jason swore he could hear the smile in her voice. "I'm just calling to remind you that you're on your own for dinner tonight."

He glanced at his calendar and nodded. "That's right. Tonight's the Great Wedding Dress Hunt."

She laughed. "It is indeed. Wish me luck!"

"Sweetheart, luck is the last thing you'll need. You'll be gorgeous no matter what you're wearing."

"Why, Sheriff," she said huskily, "with comments like that, you'll quite turn my head!"

He swiveled in his desk chair to stare out the window, imagining Kristi's face... and all the rest of her. "I certainly hope so," he said with a low growl. He swallowed and yanked his thoughts back to a more civilized level before continuing, "You have fun with Mattie and Ruby, and don't forget to eat something."

She laughed. "Don't worry, Jason. Mattie has this all planned out. We'll grab dinner somewhere and then head to *Delilah's Dresses*. I don't think I'll be late, but don't wait up."

He grinned. "Got it. Girls night out. Have fun and good hunting."

"Will do." She made a kissing sound and ended the call.

Jason sighed and turned his attention back to police work. Besides the current case, he had reports to file and budgets to review. Best get to it.

MONDAY EVENING

After closing the shop, Kristi, Mattie, and Ruby walked down the street to the newly reopened *Honey Barrel Brewpub*. When they stepped through the door, Kristi had to admit that she barely recognized the place. The new owners had removed the rough wood that had covered the walls, instead going with drywall above wainscoting. They'd chosen a deep sepia for the wainscoting and painted the drywall a much lighter golden brown. The effect was both eye-catching and restful. Kristi heartily approved. The long bar across the back of the room remained, but the huge jar of large dill pickles was gone.

Kristi shivered at that particular memory. Dill pickles had been the death of one of the former owners... at the hands of his greedy partner.

All but one of the four-top tables was full, and Kristi and her friends wasted no time settling at the remaining table.

"Good to see that the place is busy," Mattie said. "I hate to see local businesses close."

Ruby nodded. "The Williamses have done a nice job with the renovations. Everything looks so clean and fresh."

"I love the colors they've chosen," Kristi said, picking up a menu. "Now to see what kind of food they're offering."

The menu wasn't extensive, but it was certainly more varied than in the pub's last incarnation. It offered a nice selection of burgers and sandwiches, along with salads and a few sides. Kristi decided to try a small Cobb salad and a dish of baked macaroni and cheese. Ruby chose a classic hamburger and fries, while Mattie ordered a bacon cheeseburger and onion rings.

Despite the brewpub having its own signature craft beer, all three women decided to stick with water. After all, they wanted clear heads for the important business of shopping for Kristi's wedding dress.

The food was everything they'd hoped for— the Williamses had obviously hired a very talented short order cook. When the meal was finished and the waitress brought the check, Mattie grabbed it before Kristi had the chance.

"No way," Mattie said, shaking her head at Kristi's outstretched hand. "Ruby and I already discussed this. The meal is on us. Think of it as part of our gift to you."

Kristi narrowed her eyes and said, "You won't try this about the dress, right? If you think you're buying my wedding dress, I won't go along with it."

Ruby laughed, a merry, delighted sound. "Absolutely not! You're buying your own dress." She glanced at Mattie and they both giggled. "Seriously, Kristi! You don't pay us enough for anything like that, but we can afford to buy you a salad."

Kristi relaxed and grinned at her friends, who just happened to also be her employees. "Fine. Now that that's settled, thank you very much for dinner. I've enjoyed this."

While Mattie and Ruby split the bill and paid, Kristi shrugged into her down jacket and stepped outside onto the sidewalk. The sun had set while they ate and the wintry sky was clear and dark. With no clouds shadowing the moon, the stars twinkled like a scattering of tiny diamonds. She smiled, thinking of the lovely diamond ring gracing her left hand, now safely ensconced in thick woolen gloves. In just a few days, it would be joined by a wedding ring. She couldn't wait!

"Ready for the main event?" Mattie asked as she and Ruby slid into place on each side of Kristi.

"I definitely am. Let's do this!"

The three women joined arms and marched back to the quilt shop to retrieve their cars. If it had been midday, they would've walked the few blocks to *Delilah's Dresses*, but it was after dark and walking back when they finished shopping wouldn't be wise. Garnet Gateway might not be a hotbed of crime, but why tempt fate?

The dress shop's lights welcomed them as they approached the door after parking. With no other stores open, street parking had been easy to find, even for three vehicles. Mattie knocked on the door, and Delilah emerged from the dressing room and ran to open it for them.

"Mattie! Come right in," Delilah said, her blue eyes sparkling. "Hi, Ruby, and you must be Kristi... our bride." She closed the door, drew down the shades on the front windows, and turned the sign to "closed."

"Thank you so much for doing this, Delilah," Mattie said, pulling off her knit cap and gloves.

"Yes," agreed Kristi. "I really appreciate the after-hours appointment."

Delilah waved away their comments. "Think nothing of it. I love being able to work with a bride without interruption. Now, shed those coats and browse through my inventory." As they removed their outerwear, Delilah gathered the coats and hats. "I'll just put these in the back while you start your search."

Kristi gazed around at the racks of ice white gowns. Full length gowns, tea length dresses, short cocktail types. Whatever the length, the color was white, or a cream so light as to be indistinguishable from white. Some were sleek and looked like they'd hug every curve, while others had skirts so full they looked like they'd stand on their own, even if the bride fainted dead away. And the ones with cathedral length trains… she couldn't even imagine!

Kristi was just turning to Mattie, completely overwhelmed, when Delilah came back. "Mattie," she whispered, "I don't think…"

Delilah stepped forward, interrupting her. "I recognize that look," she said, patting Kristi's shoulder. "Don't worry. We'll find what you're looking for." She gestured toward a sitting area, a settee and two overstuffed chairs grouped on a lovely rose and blue patterned area rug. "Why don't we sit down. You can tell me what you envision when you think of your wedding dress."

Kristi allowed herself to be herded to the settee. Mattie settled beside her while Delilah and Ruby took the chairs.

"Now, what do you want, Kristi?"

"Certainly not any of those," she said, waving to the racks of pure white dresses. Taking a deep breath, she said, "This is a second wedding. I'm not interested in wearing white. Plus, it's a small wedding. Most of those gowns are just too... well, too much. They'd overwhelm the ceremony."

Delilah nodded. "I see. Then I have you in the wrong section of my store. Most of my mother-of-the-bride dresses wouldn't do either. Neither do you want a bridesmaid gown." She tapped a well-manicured finger against her chin while she studied Kristi. "I think I have just the thing."

Kristi started to rise, but Delilah waved her down. "No, no. Don't get up. Let me bring a few things for you to look at." And she strode away, weaving between the racks of beautiful— but totally unsuitable for Kristi— gowns.

"I hope I haven't upset her," Kristi said, glancing from Mattie to Ruby and back again. "She's been so kind to do this special appointment."

Mattie patted her hand. "Don't you worry about a thing. Delilah enjoys a challenge."

Ruby nodded. "You should've seen her with my mother and grandmother when my sister got married. She's amazing."

A few minutes later, Delilah returned, her arms draped in pastel silks. "I found these four to get us started," she said as she draped the gowns over the chair she'd been sitting in.

Picking up the first hanger, she displayed a fluffy little pink cock-tail length dress with a fitted bodice and several layers of flounces for a skirt. Glancing at Kristi's face she laughed. "Not even close, I see."

Discarding that one, she held up the next gown, a smoky gray column of tea length silk that looked like it would hug every inch of Kristi's body. Noting Kristi's expression, Delilah asked, "Is it the color or the cut you don't care for?"

Kristi pulled her gaze from the dress and met Delilah's eyes. "Both, I guess. The gray is pretty, but not for my wedding. And that looks too... form-fitting... for my taste."

Delilah nodded. "Good to know. What about this one?"

When she held up the next one, Kristi gasped. It was the most beautiful dress she'd ever seen. Even the color was perfect— gold, to highlight her hair. But not *just* gold. Like a color-wash quilt, the color flowed from palest soft yellow at the bateau neckline to a deep, burnished gold at the hemline. The dress was full length, in an a-line style, with a fitted bodice that gradually flared from waist to floor. It was exactly what Kristi wanted.

"Ah," Delilah said with a smile. "You like this one." She turned the gown so Kristi and her friends could see the back as well. "The bodice is crepe, with a bateau neckline and sheer bishop sleeves, while the back features a nice v-shape that doesn't dip too far. The lace accents on back and cuffs are beautifully done. And the skirt... well the chiffon skirt will absolutely float when you walk down the aisle."

"Delilah," Kristi breathed, reaching out to touch the cloud-soft chiffon. "It's like it was made for me! Do you have it in my size? I want to try it on."

"This one should be just right." Delilah draped the gown over one arm and pulled Kristi to standing with the other. "Come right this way." Glancing back at Mattie and Ruby, she added, "I'd suggest you two move to the viewing area. Kristi will want to use the mirrors."

Delilah accompanied Kristi into the dressing room and helped her into the gorgeous gold gown. It was a perfect fit. Even the length suited Kristi's long legs, and she decided right there and then that she'd wear comfortable, low-heeled shoes to her wedding. No fancy stiletto heels for her. She hated heels and had no intention of starting her married life trying to be someone she wasn't.

Once the final fastenings, the cuffs, were in place, Delilah guided her out of the dressing room and into the viewing area where Mattie and Ruby waited. Kristi stepped onto the low pedestal in front of triple mirrors and gasped. The gown was gorgeous, but more than that, it made Kristi look and feel beautiful! She was wearing the gown; it wasn't wearing her. An important distinction... especially for a wedding gown.

"Oh, Kristi," Mattie murmured. "That color is absolutely you! It makes your eyes sparkle and your hair shine."

"Totally," Ruby agreed. "And that's just here in the shop at the end of a long day. No make-up and your hair in a braid. Just think how you'll shine when you're all done up and focused on Jason." She sighed breathily. "It's just too romantic."

Delilah smiled. "Well, the gown has your friends' approval. What about you, Kristi? Are you satisfied, or would you like to keep looking?"

Kristi met the shop owner's gaze in the mirror. "This is the one. I can't imagine anything that would suit me better." She twisted and turned on the pedestal, looking at herself, and what was now *her* gown, from every possible angle. At last she stepped down with a nod. "If you'll help me out of this, Delilah, we'll get down to business."

"Perfect."

A surprisingly few minutes later, Kristi and Delilah concluded the sale and Delilah handed Kristi the white garment bag containing her gorgeous gold wedding gown.

"Thank you, Delilah," Kristi said as she and her friends donned their winter coats and gloves. "For the after-hours appointment, but mostly for having the perfect gown in stock."

"You're very welcome, Kristi." Delilah beamed. "I'm never sure when I add a gown to inventory whether or not it will sell, but this one," she glanced at the garment bag, "I almost feel like I picked it out just for you. Which is ridiculous, considering we hadn't met until tonight."

"Stranger things have happened," Mattie murmured and opened the door to a beautiful Montana winter night.

TUESDAY MORNING

When Sheriff Jason Reynolds stepped into the single story white stucco building that housed the sheriff's department, he was surprised to find Steve Gibbs standing at the high wooden counter that separated the public portion of the room from his team's work area. The deputy on duty at the desk nodded to Jason.

"Sheriff," he said. "Mr. Gibbs here has been waiting to see you."

Jason returned the deputy's nod and touched the brim of his Stetson in acknowledgement of the visitor. "Mr. Gibbs. What can I do for you?"

Gibbs glanced around the lobby, licked his lips, and said, "I'm in danger, Sheriff. I need protection."

Jason's eyes widened. This was a surprise. He'd expected to have to track this man down, and instead Gibbs had come to him. Keeping his expression neutral, Jason said, "Well, why don't we step through to my office so you can tell me what's got you worried?"

"Sure." Gibbs nodded and glanced again at the door as though expecting someone to come through it and drag him away. "Fine. Lead the way."

Jason strode to his office, Gibbs close on his heels. Once inside, he removed his sheepskin coat and hung it and his Stetson on the coat tree, indicating that Gibbs should do the same. Pointing to one of the chairs in front of his desk, he said, "Have a seat." Moving around the desk to his swivel chair, he sat, opened a drawer, and pulled out a small recorder. Placing it between them on the desk, Jason said, "You don't mind if I record this, do you?"

Gibbs eyed the recorder as he might a snake, but shook his head and sighed. "No, of course not. I expected as much."

Jason nodded, switched the device on, and said, "Sheriff Jason Reynolds interviewing Steve Gibbs." After adding the date and time, Jason leaned back in his chair and waved a hand toward Gibbs. "Now, Mr. Gibbs, what's on your mind?"

"Well, sir, it's like this. Ray Carrick is dead and he was one of my best bros back in the day. My other bros and I, we figure if someone knifed Ray, they might try to knife one of us next." He stopped, licked his lips, and leaned forward. "And they'd need to do it right away. I mean, me and the guys, we're only here for a few days. As soon as Turkey Day is over, we're outta here."

"I see, and you don't think whoever killed Ray could follow you back to Helena if he wanted you dead bad enough?"

Gibbs startled, narrowed his eyes, and frowned at Jason. "How do you know we live in Helena?"

Jason raised an eyebrow. "We're detectives, and you were on my list to interview today."

"What about?"

"Carrick's murder."

Gibbs gulped and sat back. "I didn't have nothing to do with Ray's murder."

"But you're worried about the person who did," Jason stated flatly. "Why don't you tell me who that is?"

Gibbs gaze flitted around the room, looking at everything except Jason.

Jason sighed. "Fine. Keep your secrets. But remember, we can't protect you if you don't tell us who you're worried about."

Still avoiding Jason's gaze, Gibbs stood, yanked his coat off the coat tree, and paused with his hands on the door knob. "Thanks for your time, Sheriff. I'll be going now."

Jason followed him out of the office and stood, fists on hips, watching as the man left the building. Janet walked over and stood beside him. "Wasn't that Steve Gibbs?"

"It was."

She cocked her head and studied Jason. "What did he want?"

"Protection." He shook his head and met his second-in-command's eyes. "But he wouldn't tell me who from."

She frowned, staring toward the front of the building. "You think he knows who killed Carrick?"

"I think he has a strong suspicion… and a reason to worry that he might be next." He sighed. "Too bad he didn't trust me enough to share what he knows. Or thinks he knows."

She nodded. "Maybe Jennings or Atwood will be more talkative."

"That would be good. For them as well as us." He paused for a moment, glanced across the work area to where the murder board stood, and then said, "Why don't you take Eric and go talk to Jennings and Atwood. Let me know what you find out."

"No problem. What are you going to do?"

He rubbed a hand across his forehead. "I've got reports to finish if I'm going to manage to take that honeymoon I promised Kristi."

Janet laughed. "No 'if' about that, Sheriff. Not if you want to have a peaceful rest of your life."

He smiled. "You're right about that." He turned to return to his office. "Good hunting. I hope one of those two gives us a new lead."

"No worries, sir. If they know anything, Lawson and I will ferret it out." She turned toward the work area. "Eric! You're with me and we're in the field."

Jason dropped into his desk chair and stared out the window for a moment before grabbing a stack of papers and pulling them to the center of his work space. Paperwork. The bane of his existence, but a necessary part of the job.

TUESDAY AFTERNOON

Right after lunch, Kristi gave each of her cats a final pat before jumping in her bright red Subaru Outback and heading to Billings. Her parents' flight was due in a little over two and a half hours, giving Kristi just enough time to drive to Billings, wind her way up onto the rimrocks above the city, park, and meet them at the baggage carousel.

Entering the airport, she studied the overhead information display and then raced to the baggage claim assigned to her parents' flight. Heart hammering, she skidded to a halt at the empty area. No passengers milled about and no luggage circled on the conveyor belt. Evidently, she wasn't late.

Too excited to sit, she paced. She hadn't seen her parents for several years. Not since they retired to Sedona, Arizona. They talked on the phone regularly and even managed a video call every now and then, but there was nothing like getting together in person.

Why, the last time she'd been able to hug her mom, she'd still been married to Jason!

Now, Kristi had not only been divorced for nearly three years, but she'd bought a business, remodeled it, and had it up and running successfully for more than a year and a half. Her life had changed dramatically in the time they'd been gone, and now, it was about to change again. Kristi and Jason were getting married again… and this time both of them were a lot wiser and definitely more committed to each other. This time around, they'd give their relationship the attention it deserved.

And both sets of their parents would be here to witness their wedding—the formal declaration of their union.

She'd just about decided to sit down when a horn blared and the conveyor belt began to move. A moment later, passengers sifted into the area, dragging rolling carry-on bags behind them. Kristi craned her neck looking for familiar faces.

Suddenly, they appeared. Her father's graying hair and horn-rimmed glasses clearly visible above the heads of the passengers crowded around him. Good thing he was so tall. It made spotting him so much easier than finding her little mother. And then the crowd shifted, and there was her mother, right beside Dad as always, her gaze eagerly searching the sea of faces.

Kristi squealed and raced to hug them. First Mom, then Dad, then all three of them were a tangle of limbs embracing each other and laughing until they nearly cried.

"You're here," Kristi exclaimed. "I can hardly believe it."

Mom caught Kristi's face in her hands and stared lovingly into her eyes. "We wouldn't be anywhere else."

Dad kissed Kristi's cheek. "Let me look at you! You look wonderful. Life must be treating you right."

Kristi beamed at them both. "Now that you're here, everything is perfect."

Her mother, Elizabeth Lundrigan, waited by the seating area with their carry-on bags while Kristi and her father, Edward, squeezed into place by the baggage conveyor to watch for their luggage. Kristi fairly hummed with happiness at having her parents so close again.

They hadn't changed a bit. Elizabeth, or Beth as she preferred, was a petite woman, her dark hair now streaked with silver and her figure a bit plumper than it had been when Kristi was a child, but she bloomed with health and good-nature, as she always had. Beth had always been a calming influence on everyone who knew her. She oozed comfort and confidence, as though she simply knew that everything would turn out for the best.

Edward, Ed to friends and family, was Beth's rock. Her stalwart defender— not that Kristi's mom ever needed defending, not when everyone who met her loved her instantly!— her knight in shining armor. At six foot four, he towered over his petite wife, and while he'd never been called upon to bear the weight of armor or wield a sword, he was still in excellent physical condition. Ed's hair had gone completely gray and it seemed to Kristi that his signature horn-rimmed glasses had thicker lenses than she remembered, but other than that her dad appeared unchanged.

Taller than her mother, but nowhere near as tall as her dad, Kristi had inherited her blonde hair and blue eyes from her father. Though Mom liked to say Kristi's coloring was a throw-back to Beth's mother, Kristi's beloved Nanna Van Oss. The very same grandmother whose gracious gift of inheritance had allowed Kristi to buy *Delectable Mountain Quilting*.

Once the luggage had been retrieved and loaded into Kristi's Outback, the three enjoyed a very pleasant drive back to Garnet Gateway, catching up on family news and marveling at the lack of snow so late in November.

As they pulled into the driveway, Kristi's mother exclaimed, "What a lovely home, Kristi, and you have such a nice view of the 'Sorkees!"

"Thanks," Kristi said, popping the hatch so they could retrieve the luggage. "That view was what sold me on this house. Come on in so I can show you around."

Juggling bags, she unlocked the front door and ushered her parents into the living room, where they were immediately greeted by Stitches and Between. Fortunately, the kitty-kids waited until Beth and Ed put their luggage down before they began to wind around their ankles.

"And who are these?" Beth asked with a smile as she leaned down to stroke Between's back.

"That's Between," Kristi said, pointing to the little black and white tuxedo cat. "And that's Stitches," she continued, pointing to the gray tabby winding around her dad's ankles.

Dad reached down and picked Stitches up, careful to support her hind quarters. "Well, hello there, Stitches. Nice to meet you."

Stitches responded by purring loudly.

Kristi laughed. "I think she likes you."

"We can't leave you out, Between. Come here." Mom picked the little male up and cuddled him.

Not to be outdone, Between began to purr and patted Beth's cheek with a paw, his claws carefully retracted.

"It's official," Kristi said. "You've been accepted into the family."

"Well, thank goodness," Mom said with a laugh. "Where did you come up with those names?"

Kristi shrugged. "Quilting terms. Stitches doesn't need an explanation, but a between is the very short, very sharp needle used in hand quilting. When he shows his claws, you'll understand the reference."

"This is all very nice," Dad said to Stitches, "but we should put our luggage away." He glanced up at Kristi. "And then we need a tour of the house."

"Great idea," Kristi said, picking up a suitcase. "Follow me."

Reluctantly, Ed and Beth deposited the cats on the couch and gathered the rest of their baggage.

Kristi provided an abbreviated tour as they walked. "This is the dining room. The kitchen's right through there. The bedrooms are down this hall. This is my sewing room. That's the master bedroom—with its own bath, and here's the guest bath. And finally, the guest room, which is yours for the duration."

"What a lovely room," Beth said, dropping her suitcase and walking to one of the windows. "Oh, look, Ed. She has an oak tree in the backyard!"

Ed joined his wife at the window and nodded. "Good sized yard too." He turned to Kristi. "Good job on your real estate purchase. Can't wait to see the business you bought."

Kristi grinned. "And I can't wait to show it to you!"

Beth turned, a small frown creasing her forehead. "What about Jason's parents? Where will they stay?"

"Jason has a small apartment near his office, but his folks will be staying at the Garnet Gateway Inn." Kristi gulped, suddenly nervous. "I could probably get you a room there too, if you'd prefer. I just thought…"

"No!" Beth interrupted, rushing to Kristi's side. "We'd much rather be here with you."

"This is perfect, sweetheart," Dad said, joining his wife and daughter in another group hug. "We wouldn't want to stay anywhere else."

Kristi sighed happily, content to be held in her parents' arms.

18

TUESDAY EVENING

Jason smiled fondly as he stared across the dining table at his parents. He hadn't managed to find the time to drive to Billings to pick them up, but had instead sent a deputy, Evan Knott, to the airport to retrieve them. His schedule simply hadn't allowed it. Instead, he'd spent the afternoon pouring over his deputies' reports on their interviews with Jennings and Atwood as well as studying the details of Jerry Wanamaker's death. There was a connection there, he could almost smell it, but so far he hadn't been able to ferret out the link that connected Wanamaker and Carrick. Other than carousel horses, that is.

But now, now he could relax and enjoy this time with family. His family. For once again, Ed and Beth Lundrigan were about to be part of that family.

The six of them sat around Kristi's dining table enjoying a wonderful takeout meal of Rizzoli's lasagna, focaccia bread, tossed salad, and a nice bottle of chianti.

The six of them. Together again. He and Kristi. Ed and Beth. Reggie and Mamie.

He grinned and forked up another bite of baked pasta oozing with cheese and perfectly spiced beef as Kristi chattered happily about the venue Stacy had found for their wedding. She described the conference room on the second floor of the Garnet Gateway Inn while both sets of parents oohed and aahed appropriately. Especially Reggie and Mamie as they had checked into a room in that very inn just a few hours ago.

He glanced at his father, Reginald— Reggie here in a family setting— Reynolds was an old-fashioned lawman. He'd been chief of police in Butte when Jason was growing up and had instilled in his son a love of the law and a deep seated dedication to duty and protecting people. Even the bad guys. Reggie had always been careful to see that those he arrested were fairly treated and that they were given every opportunity to show their remorse and mend their ways. Traits Jason worked to emulate to this day.

His father wasn't an imposing man, Jason was taller and more muscular than his dad had ever been, but Reggie held himself with confidence and dignity and his dark blue eyes could practically compel a man to tell the truth. It had been a sad day in Butte when Reggie had announced his retirement and his intention to move to Boulder, Colorado for its far milder weather.

He glanced fondly at his mother. Mamie, or more formally Mary Catherine, was a perfect mother as far as Jason was concerned. She'd never complained about his father's unpredictable schedule, but had provided a stable and loving home for the family. Mamie, always a little plump, had gained weight since their retirement to Colorado, but Jason agreed with his father's comment that there was simply more of her to love these days. Her wavy chestnut hair had turned suddenly white a few years back, but the change agreed with her, giving her an almost regal appearance.

The dinner discussion had turned to Kristi's wedding gown and Jason's attention perked up when his mom asked when they could see it.

"On Saturday, of course," Kristi said with a laugh. "It's a secret until then, but let me just say, it's perfect and I'm thrilled to have found it."

"At least tell us the color," Beth begged. "Did you go with white again?"

"Definitely not," Kristi said with a bit of an eye roll. "Okay. I can give you that much. It's gold." She sighed happily. "An absolutely beautiful gold."

Jason reached for her hand and squeezed when she met his halfway. "Guess your shopping trip with Mattie and Ruby was successful."

She smiled dreamily. "Better than I could possibly have hoped."

Reggie lifted his wineglass. "To Jason and Kristi," he said, "may they live happily ever after."

"Hear, hear!" exclaimed Ed as all four parents raised their glasses and sipped.

Jason leaned over and kissed Kristi's cheek, then smiled at the others. "Thank you, and thank you all for making the effort to be here with us."

"We wouldn't have missed it for the world," Beth said.

"And we're thrilled that we get to spend Thanksgiving with you as well," said Mamie. "This is definitely going to be a week to remember!"

When they finished dinner, everyone pitched in for the cleanup. Kristi's small kitchen felt a bit overcrowded with six adults carrying in dishes, putting leftovers away, and rinsing and loading the dishwasher, but everyone was good-natured about ducking out of each other's way.

They were just about to head to living room to sit and chat when Jason's phone rang. He excused himself and answered.

"Sheriff Reynolds."

"Sorry to bother you, Sheriff," Clara said, "but you're needed at the carousel." She paused, and Jason heard her draw a deep breath. "There's been another murder."

———

JASON STARED at the body of a man he'd never met. He recognized him though. His picture was tacked to the murder board in the station's workroom. Billy Jennings.

The body was arranged too similarly to how Ray Carrick's had been to be coincidence. Jennings slumped in the corner of the same chariot bench, his eyes open, but glazed in death. He'd also been stabbed twice, once in the belly and once in the chest. Jason expected the coroner to find that the wounds came from two different knives and were likely delivered by two different hands.

Shaking his head, Jason studied the scene. It might have been Ray Carrick's death scene. The similarities were too pronounced, the differences minor: time of day and the victim's name. He was profoundly glad that Kristi was nowhere near the scene this time.

She'd been so happy at dinner with their parents. He didn't want anything to mar that happiness. Especially not murder.

Janet Millson joined him. "Well, that's one suspect we can strike from our list."

Jason gave her a sidelong glance. "True enough, and unless Steve Gibbs has Oscar-worthy acting talents, I think he's off the list as well. His fear was too pronounced to be faked." He stared out into the darkness, beyond the glare of the lights the crime scene techs had set up, before glancing at his second-in-command again. "What about Atwood. Think he might be capable of this?"

Janet considered, but shook her head. "Frankly, he didn't seem capable of much of anything. If he's involved in drug trafficking, it's because Jennings or Gibbs told him exactly what to do and where to do it." She shrugged. "He's currently employed as a stock boy in a grocery store, and it sounds like that may be the pinnacle of his career path."

"Well, bring him in anyway," Jason said. "We may want to hold him in protective custody. He could be next on the murderer's list."

"We can do that," she said, "but he's home for the holiday and his folks won't be happy if we hold him on Thursday."

Jason studied the body and nodded toward it. "They'll be a whole lot less happy if he ends up like that."

Janet sighed. "True enough."

19

WEDNESDAY MORNING

Kristi stepped carefully over the cats on the way to her kitchen. "Honestly, kitty-kids. You should really stay out of the kitchen today… and tomorrow. I promise you'll get your treats, but we're going to be busy and stepping over you is just going to slow everyone down."

At an amused chuckle, she turned to find her mother grinning at her. "Like they're going to mind you," Beth said, shaking her head. "Unless you plan to put them in a kennel, we'll all just have to be wary of them."

Kristi sighed. "No. Of course I'm not going to pen them up, but they are likely to be a nuisance."

As if in agreement, Between meowed loudly.

Kristi shook a finger at him. "That'll be quite enough out of you." She turned her attention to Beth. "Where's Dad?"

"He borrowed your car and headed out to spend the day with Reggie," she said. "He didn't want to be in the way."

Kristi nodded. "Excellent plan."

"Are we expecting Mamie?"

"Yes. Originally Jason was going to drop her off on his way into work, but…. Well, you might as well know. There was another murder last night. He went in too early to drive his mom over."

"Oh, no!" Beth exclaimed. "That's terrible. Anyone you knew?"

"No," Kristi said quietly. Still, Jason's call last night had brought her memories of finding the body on the carousel back with a vengeance. She preferred not to think about it. She shook her head. Good thing she wasn't one of Jason's deputies. Marrying the sheriff was as close to law enforcement as she wanted to get.

"My friend Stacy is coming over to help us cook. She'll stop by and pick up Mamie. I called them both earlier to make the arrangements." She smiled, thoughts of Stacy brightening her mood. "You'll love Stacy, Mom. She and her husband Mark will be joining us for the big meal tomorrow, so this will give you a chance to get to know her beforehand."

Kristi was pulling plates and serving dishes out of her cupboards and Beth was peeling potatoes when the doorbell rang.

"I'll get it," Kristi called as her mother dried her hands on a kitchen towel. Racing to the front door (while avoiding the cats!) Kristi yanked it open to find Stacy and Mamie on the other side.

"Welcome," she called and stood aside while the two women entered, shed their coats, and hung them on the nearby coat tree.

Hugging Stacy, she said, "Thanks so much for bringing Mamie over."

"No problem," Stacy said with a laugh. "And you must be Beth." She disentangled herself from Kristi and stepped to greet her friend's mom. "Mamie told me all about you on the way over."

Beth shook Stacy's hand, but glanced at Mamie. "Only good things, I hope!"

Mamie's eyes widened. "Why, Beth! I only know good things about you." She gave a very theatrical gasp, and continued, "Do you have a dark side? Tell me everything!"

Everyone laughed and they headed toward the kitchen.

"I have to warn you, my kitty-kids are overexcited today, so be aware of your feet… especially if you're carrying anything hot."

Stacy smiled. "We'll try really hard not to cook your cats, Kristi."

"Especially you," Kristi said, narrowing her eyes at her friend. "No mishaps with my cat-sitter just before the honeymoon!"

"I wondered who was going to watch over these two sweeties while you and Jason are away," Beth said, leaning down to give each of the cats an under-chin scritch. She glanced up at Stacy. "So you're the lucky person."

"Yes, indeed," Stacy said, smiling. "Stitches and Between and I go way back. Kristi and I were just getting to know each other when I fell for her cats."

Kristi nodded. "Remember when I was hospitalized a couple of years ago?"

"You mean when you were shot?" Beth asked, her eyes wide.

"Well, yes," Kristi admitted. "Anyway, Stacy took care of the kitty-kids while I was laid up."

"Shot?" asked Mamie. "When did this happen?"

Kristi waved the question away. "Ancient history. Let's focus on the now."

Beth sidled over to Mamie. "Don't worry," she said in a none-too-quiet whisper. "I'll tell you all about it later."

They all got to work. While Mamie and Beth peeled potatoes and sweet potatoes… and whispered about Kristi's brush with a bullet, Kristi and Stacy added leaves to the dining table, found the tablecloth and set the table with Kristi's best china. They even placed the large platter and serving dishes in the center just so they had an idea what would fit on the table tomorrow.

"Are you going to have a centerpiece?" Stacy asked.

Kristi shook her head. "I figure the food, especially the turkey, is enough of a centerpiece. Flowers would just take up space."

Stacy nodded. "I know Mark and Jason will be more interested in the food than they would be in flowers." They laughed.

As much as Kristi loved her mom and Jason's mom, it was good to have a friend with her. She and Stacy had grown close since Stacy had acted as her realtor and helped her buy *Delectable Mountain Quilting*. Friendship was a beautiful thing.

By lunch time they had the potatoes and sweet potatoes chopped and in bags in the refrigerator and two pies in the oven. One pecan pie and one pumpkin pie. Kristi and Stacy assembled ham and cheese sandwiches, sliced apples, and iced tea, and the four women took their plates to the living room for a well-deserved break.

"So what else do we need to do in advance?" Stacy asked after sipping her tea.

Kristi swallowed a bite of her sandwich. "The turkey is prepped and waiting in the garage refrigerator. The pies are baking. The potatoes and sweet potatoes are ready to be cooked tomorrow. I think that just leaves the cranberry relish and assembling the sage and sausage stuffing." She turned to her mom. "Do you think of anything else?"

"Not really," Beth said, wiping her lips with her napkin. "I mean, we could do the rolls, but I think we'd be better to wait until tomorrow for those. What do you think, Mamie?"

Jason's mother nodded. "I agree. We should bake the rolls tomorrow." She took another bite of sandwich, swallowed and asked, "What kind of cranberry relish are you thinking of?"

Kristi smiled at her mother. "We have a wonderful family recipe from Nanna Van Oss for cranberry orange relish. You'll love it."

Stacy laughed. "I'll give it a try. I grew up on the canned, jellied stuff… which I hate! If Mark likes yours, I'll have to wheedle the recipe out of you."

"Absolutely," Beth said. "Anyone who takes care of my grand-kitties is family, so you're entitled to the recipe."

They laughed, but Kristi's thoughts turned to Jason. She hoped his day was going well, and that murder would allow him a day off to enjoy tomorrow's feast.

The four women finished their lunch just as the timer sounded for the pies in the oven.

"Well," Mamie said, standing and heading to the kitchen. "I guess that's the signal for us to get back to work."

Kristi and Stacy washed and dried the dishes they'd used for lunch while Mamie and Beth pulled the pies from the oven and placed them on trivets in the center of the dining table to cool.

The house smelled wonderful! Kristi smiled. Thanksgiving was off to a great start.

20

WEDNESDAY AFTERNOON

Jason had been surprised to get a phone call from his dad inviting him to lunch.

"Come on, boy," Reggie had wheedled. "Ed and I are on our own and we don't know our way around town the way you do."

"Why are you on your own?" Jason had asked. "Where is Kristi? What about Mom and Mrs. Lundrigan?"

He'd practically been able to see his dad throw up his hands. "The women are all busy with baking and getting ready for tomorrow's feast. Us men are on our own. Now, are you with us or not?"

Jason had glanced at his murder board and made a snap decision. He was spinning his wheels. Maybe a break with his dad and his almost father-in-law would help pull him out of his rut. "Fine. I'll meet you at *Roasted Beans*. It's on Main, just a few doors down from my office. Think you can find it?"

"You bet. We'll be there in just a couple of minutes."

Jason had already ordered coffee and was sitting at a four-top table near the window when the two men entered.

"Huh," his dad said, sliding into the chair across from Jason. "A coffee shop." He glanced around. "This is what passes for a diner in this town?"

Ed seated himself and looked around approvingly. "Nice and clean," he said. "Most of the tables are full. Must have decent food or the locals wouldn't eat here."

A waitress appeared with a tray of white porcelain mugs. "Howdy, Sheriff. Here's that coffee you ordered. I know yours is black, who gets the cream, no sugar?" When Reggie raised his hand, she placed a mug in front of him, then smiled at Ed. "That must mean the cream and sugar is yours."

Ed smiled. "Sure does. Thank you."

She lowered the tray and glanced at each of the men. "Now, we don't usually take orders from the tables— folk usually order food at the counter when they order their coffee— but I can make an exception for you three if you know what you'd like."

"Menu?" asked Reggie.

She pointed to the large blackboard behind and above the counter. "We have some great bakery goods, but if you're looking for lunch, it's pretty much sandwiches."

Ed squinted at the board, then gave up and smiled at the young woman again. "That's a bit distant for my eyes. I don't suppose you can find me a ham and cheese on whole wheat?"

"You bet," she said with a smile. "Lettuce and tomato? Mustard or mayo?"

"All of the above," Ed said, nodding.

She turned to Reggie. "And you, sir?"

"How about roast beef with cheddar, maybe a slice of bacon, and all the fixings."

She nodded. "No problem. Sheriff?"

"I'll have my regular, Jenny," he said. "And thanks for helping us out."

"Anytime, Sheriff." She turned to return to the kitchen, but said over her shoulder, "You and your deputies are some of our best customers."

"Eat here often, do you?" asked Reggie.

"Practically every day," Jason answered after sipping his coffee. "But usually not in person."

Ed cocked his head and raised an eyebrow. "How does that work?"

Jason shrugged. "Clara, our dispatcher, usually calls in an order for everyone who wants something and one of my deputies comes and picks it up. The department runs a tab, and my chief deputy sees that it's paid every Friday." He drank more coffee. "The system works for us."

"You buy your deputies lunch every day?" Reggie looked aghast. "My old department would've never done anything like that!"

Jason grinned. "Did I say Janet paid out of our budget? Nope. We keep a petty cash box. Everyone who gets lunch pays into petty cash, and on Friday, Janet calls, gets the total for the week and brings the cash over. Everyone eats. Everyone pays. And a local business is supported." He shrugged. "It's convenient, and it works. We'll pay the normal way today, and it's my treat."

"Hey now," said Reggie, just as Jenny arrived with their sandwiches. "That's hardly fair. I'm the one who invited you out to lunch."

Jenny set the plates in front of them, smiled, and said, "You gentlemen enjoy your lunch." She glanced at Jason, and said more quietly, "If you need anything, just let me know."

Jason nodded. "Thanks, Jenny. This looks great. The only thing we'll need is the check after a while. Bring it to me, please."

"Will do." She smiled and walked away.

Reggie huffed, but Ed studied Jason's plate. "We never asked. What's your sandwich?"

"Peanut butter and honey with two strips of crisp bacon." He picked up his sandwich and took a bite, ignoring Ed's surprised expression.

Reggie shook his head. "Seriously? You're still eating those? And in public?" He sighed. "I thought you outgrew that combination years ago."

Jason grinned and toasted his dad with his coffee. "Nope. Still one of my favorites. And Jenny makes it just right."

The two older men dug into their sandwiches as well and conversation ceased while their food was consumed with much appreciation.

———

AFTER LUNCH, Jason sent his out-of-town guests off to the historical society while he returned to work. He stood studying the murder board when his second-in-command, Janet Millson, joined him.

"I can't help but think the Wanamaker death is the key," she said. "What do you think?"

Jason nodded. "I expected one of the three old friends to be the killer, but with one dead, one scared out of his mind, and the remaining one not the brightest bulb in the house, I think we need a new angle." He turned to face Janet. "Want to go with me to interview Jerry Wanamaker's dad?"

"Let's. Since his only brother is in prison up in Deer Lodge, it's his dad or nothing."

"Grab your gear. We'll take my Trail Blazer."

Jason parked his vehicle in front of the Wanamaker home and the two of them walked to the front door. Janet knocked, and after a few moments, the door opened to reveal a man in his mid-forties wearing faded jeans and a red and black plaid flannel shirt with the sleeves rolled up to the elbows. His hair was disheveled and he was in need of a shave, but his eyes were wary.

"What do you want?" he asked, looking Jason up and down before turning his attention to Janet. "I didn't call for the law."

"I'm Sheriff Reynolds," Jason said. "This is Chief Deputy Millson. We have a few questions for you, Mr. Wanamaker. May we come in?"

"Not interested in what you want," the man said and started to swing the door shut.

Janet stopped the door with her boot. "We're going to ask those questions, sir. It's your choice whether we do it here or in an interview room at the station."

"What'll it be?" Jason asked.

Wanamaker swung the door open again. "By all means, Sheriff, come right in," he sneered. "Would you like some tea and crumpets?"

Jason ignored the sarcastic tone, but stepped inside the residence. He glanced around, quickly taking in the lay of the land. The man lived like a pig. Half-eaten food rested on surfaces that hadn't been cleaned in who knew when. Papers littered the floor and chairs were covered in trash and empty beer bottles. The place smelled like rotting food and stale beer.

He'd seen worse, Jason decided, but not by much. At least the place didn't smell like piss or vomit. Jason removed his Stetson, as did Janet, but neither chose to sit. Wanamaker dropped onto the sprung cushions of his couch.

"What's so important that you'd come here and harass me in my home?"

No point in beating around the bush, Jason thought. "Where were you early Saturday morning?" he asked.

Wanamaker blinked. "Saturday? I was in Deer Lodge. It was my weekend to visit Joey. I drove over on Friday, spent the weekend there."

Janet made a note, while Jason continued. "Your son, Joey Wanamaker, is incarcerated in the prison at Deer Lodge."

"That's right. You should know. You didn't lock him up, but the State troopers said they notified you."

Jason nodded. "They did. And you were there all weekend? Where did you stay?"

"At that little motel out on the highway. The closest one to the prison." He frowned. "What's this all about?"

Jason ignored the question. "And what about last night? Where were you between eight p.m. and midnight?"

Wanamaker stood. "I was at the Rodeo Bar and Grill. I worked the grill until 10:00, then stuck around for a few drinks with friends until closing."

"What time is closing?" Janet asked, still jotting down notes.

"Depends on what time the place empties out. Last night it was about 1:30 a.m."

"Names of your friends?" Janet asked. Wanamaker listed off four men, all of them known to the sheriff's department.

Jason nodded and turned toward the door. "Thank you for your time, Mr. Wanamaker." He reached for the door knob, paused, and turned back to face the man. "Any thoughts about how and why your younger son died?"

Anger flared in Wanamaker's eyes. "Why? No one bothered to ask when it happened."

"I'm asking now."

"And I'm telling you, my Jerry was murdered. No way he ODed. Sure, he took a taste now and then, but he was into sales, not using. Someone injected him and left him to die on that carousel."

Jason studied the man and then asked, "Who do you think might have done such a thing?"

Wanamaker shrugged and dropped back onto the couch. "I don't know. A relative of a client would be my guess, but I wasn't involved in Jerry's business. Didn't know who he sold to."

"Not the client himself?" Janet asked.

"Why? They were happy. They were getting what they wanted from Jerry. No reason to kill him." He rubbed a hand over his eyes. "What do you want to bring Jerry's death up for? Everything went to hell when Rosie died. First her, then Jerry, now Joey's in prison. Everything's gone to hell." He leaned his head against the back of the couch and closed his eyes.

Jason pulled the door open and he and Janet stepped out, leaving the man to his grief.

WEDNESDAY EVENING

"I kind of miss Reggie and Mamie tonight," Ed said as he helped Beth set the folding table up in the living room. Kristi's dining table was already set for tomorrow's big meal, so the three of them would be making do with the white-topped plastic version for tonight's dinner. "Jason, too, of course," he added quickly hoping not to rouse his daughter's ire.

But Kristi just laughed. "Jason and I decided we each needed one dinner alone with our own parents." She frowned. "Though I'm not sure Reggie and Mamie will get as much of his attention as they deserve."

Beth nodded, returning to the kitchen to gather plates and silverware. "He did seem a bit preoccupied when he stopped by to pick Mamie up." She glanced at her husband as Ed came in to carry the platter of cornbread and cheeses to the table. "Did you and Reggie have a nice day? You left him at the Inn, right?"

He kissed her cheek and hurried toward the table. "Of course I left him at the Inn," he called over his shoulder. "What did you think? That I'd abandon him somewhere downtown? Jason's mood had nothing to do with me."

"Of course not," Kristi said as she ladled beef stew into soup bowls from the crockpot where it had been simmering all afternoon. "He's just preoccupied with these murders. If he has to leave them to his deputies to solve, he will. But he won't be happy about it." She rested the ladle on the rim of the crockpot and closed her eyes. "I won't be a bit surprised to hear he takes time for a nice dinner with his folks, and then leaves them at the Inn to return to the office for a few hours. I just hope he can take time to relax tomorrow.

"Speaking of nice dinners, I'd say we're about ready to eat this one."

Kristi gave herself a mental pat on the back for remembering to start the easy recipe in the midst of all the prepping for tomorrow's Thanksgiving feast. As always, the stew smelled like it had turned out perfectly. The hearty blend of potatoes, carrots, celery, broth, herbs, and spices was winter comfort food at its finest.

When everything had been transported to their temporary table, she and her parents pulled straight-backed chairs from the dining room and sat down to enjoy their meal.

"Delicious," Ed said after a few bites of stew. "I'm amazed you had time to think about dinner with all the other cooking you ladies did today."

"That's the beauty of a slow cooker," Beth said. "You assemble the meal and forget it until you're ready to eat."

Kristi nodded, buttering a piece of cornbread. She held it up and said, "This was the hardest part. Remembering to put the batter in the oven."

Beth bit into her piece of cornbread, chewed and swallowed. "Well, I for one, am glad you remembered. I haven't had cornbread in far too long… and it goes perfectly with the stew."

Kristi and her parents spent the rest of the meal catching up on their busy lives. Ed and Beth regaled Kristi with tales of their new home in Sedona, Arizona, a very different place than their Montana roots, while Kristi brought them up to date on her involvement in Jason's last two murder cases.

"Good heavens," said Beth. "Who would've thought this little town would have so much crime?"

"Well, I'm glad you're staying out of this one," Ed said. "My little girl has no business sticking her nose into murder investigations."

"Dad!" Kristi exclaimed, stung by the accusation. "I didn't *stick my nose in*! I just happened to find evidence and then get caught by the killer before I could pass it along to Jason. SO not my fault!"

Ed frowned and pointed his spoon at her. "Well, just see that you leave the investigating to your husband in the future."

Kristi rolled her eyes, but didn't respond, choosing to scoop up another spoonful of stew instead.

Beth glanced from daughter to husband, sighed, and said, "So, tell us more about Stacy and this husband of hers. Did you say his name was Mark?"

Trust, Mom, Kristi thought. *Always the peacemaker.*

The rest of the meal passed in Kristi's tales of purchasing *Delectable Mountain Quilting* (without further references to the body she found at the back door!), its renovation, opening, and the women she'd hired to help her with the business. Since Kristi was proud of what she'd accomplished with the quilt shop, the evening passed in happy, upbeat conversation.

Once the kitchen was cleaned, the leftovers added to the garage refrigerator, and the folding table put away, Kristi wished her parents a good night. The day had been exhausting, and she practically fell into bed. She missed the comfort of Jason's warm body beside her, but Stitches and Between did their best to take his place. Both cats curled up next to her, purring their little hearts out. Company was fine, but they, like Kristi, missed their quiet routine.

And tomorrow would be even less routine than today had been.

Kristi stroked the cats and closed her eyes. She'd need her rest for the coming day! She could only hope Jason would find time to rest as well.

22

THANKSGIVING MORNING

Jason allowed himself a slow start to his morning. He wanted to rush to the office so he could pull the files and evidence the department had collected regarding Jerry Wanamaker's death, but he forced himself to slow down. To remember that his folks were in town for a very limited time, and that once the reception was over on Saturday, he and Kristi would leave on their honeymoon. He should take every opportunity he could to spend time with his parents.

With that in mind, he joined them for breakfast at the Inn.

Sure his dad, a former police officer himself, would understand if Jason begged off, but that didn't make it right. Besides, his mother might be accustomed to being relegated to second place behind an investigation, but he wasn't his dad. Plus, Jason appreciated seeing the light sparkle in her eyes when he joined them at their table and kissed her cheek.

He needed to remember that light and make sure he never extinguished it from Kristi's eyes.

So he enjoyed his eggs Benedict, made small talk with his folks, and when they'd finished their meal, delivered them to Kristi's home with a promise to return well before the scheduled 2:00 p.m. dinner time.

Before pulling out of Kristi's driveway to head to the department, he called Janet Millson. "Have you pulled Wanamaker's files and evidence out of storage yet?" he asked as soon as she picked up.

"I did," she said. "First thing this morning."

"Great," he said. "That's one stop I won't have to make."

"Are you headed in?"

"I am. We'll comb through his books and see if we can cross-reference any names we find with crimes in the area."

"Sounds good. I'll get started. See you when you get here."

"That you will," Jason said, and clicked off.

By noon he and Janet had assembled a fairly detailed list of Jerry Wanamaker's clients. Jason glanced at his second-in-command and said, "We might want to follow up with the ones of these who are still in Garnet County. See if they're still using and who their supplier might be."

Janet nodded. "Sounds like a great project for the deputies to work on while you're otherwise occupied." She raised her eyebrows and grinned mischievously.

"Funny. But that only works if we close the murder cases before I leave."

"True," she said, picking up their list and moving to the computer. "On to the second part of our search: cross-referencing with known crimes."

Jason frowned. "Let's start with deaths, especially overdose deaths. Jerry could've been killed as vengeance for a loved one's death. If someone died of an OD, a relative could've decided Jerry was responsible. No drugs, no death."

She typed criteria into a search bar as she spoke. "I can see someone making that connection, possibly acting on it, but I'm not sure I see how that connects to Ray Carrick or Billy Jennings."

"If we find a connection to Wanamaker, maybe we'll discover the connection to Carrick and his erstwhile friends."

An hour later they had a list of drug related charges, most of which had resulted in stints of community service and / or psychiatric counseling. No deaths by overdose. Not a single one. They did find one unrelated death. A young woman— really only a girl since she was still in her teens at time of death— had committed suicide. No drug use was noted in the coroner's report.

"Okay," Jason said with a sigh. "That theory's a bust. Got any other ideas?"

"Right now, my main thought is that if we miss our respective Thanksgiving dinners, we're going to be in deep doo-doo."

Jason glanced at his watch and grimaced. "You are on the nose, as usual." He grabbed his shearling coat and Stetson off the coat tree and shrugged into them. "If I'm late, you might not have to worry about me leaving for my honeymoon. Kristi might decide to call off the wedding."

Janet laughed. "I seriously doubt that. But why risk it? See you tomorrow."

Jason yanked the door open and, waving over his shoulder,

dashed for his Trail Blazer. Good thing Janet had been paying attention to the time!

23

THANKSGIVING NOON

Kristi dried her hands on a kitchen towel and paused to appreciate her helpers. Stacy and Mark had come early to help out, and she'd assigned Mark the task of keeping her dad and Jason's dad entertained until it was their turn in the kitchen. They were camped out in the living room watching something on television. Parades. Sports. Dog shows. She didn't care what as long as they stayed out of the way.

Her kitchen was too small to accommodate too many cooks at once.

Beth and Mamie bustled around making sure all the last minute preparations were in order. Both women were old hands at putting Thanksgiving meals together, often for a lot more than eight people. Kristi and Stacy jumped in to do whatever was needed.

Leaning against the counter for a moment, Kristi ran through the menu. The turkey was roasting. Check. She'd timed the roasting so that it could come out of the oven at one o'clock and have an hour to rest before serving.

The cranberry sauce was ready and waiting in the garage refrigerator. Check. The sage and sausage stuffing would go into the oven as soon as the turkey came out, along with the green bean casserole and the sweet potatoes. The oven would be full, but everything should just fit.

The pies were ready for dessert, and Reggie would whip up the garlic mashed potatoes while Ed made the gravy. Mamie and Beth would move the food into serving dishes while Kristi and Stacy delivered those dishes to the table.

And Mark? Well, he and Jason would be in charge of carving the turkey. They would load a serving platter with slices ready to be placed on plates.

Whew! Thanksgiving dinner was moving along just as planned.

Now, all they needed was Jason!

Kristi glanced at the front door. No Jason. No worries. He'd be here before it was time to sit down. She knew he would. He might be busy tracking down a killer, but he wouldn't forget Thanksgiving dinner.

Would he?

She shook her head. Of course he wouldn't. She was worrying for no reason. And she didn't have time to worry today. There were things to be done.

Pasting a smile on her face, she nodded to Stacy and they carried trays of snacks to the men in the living room.

"Now don't go overboard," she said as she placed a tray of sliced fresh vegetables along with a bowl of dip on the coffee table. "You all have work to do, but this should tide you over until it's your turn in the kitchen."

Stacy set a pitcher of iced tea and glasses beside the vegetables. "Enjoy," she said with a smile.

Mark grinned. "Thanks, Babe." He grabbed a carrot stick, dragged it through the creamy dip, and popped it in his mouth. "Kristi, everything smells wonderful. Can't wait for Jason to get here so we can carve that turkey."

By 1:30 p.m., Kristi was starting to worry. The food was right on schedule. They'd be able to sit down at two o'clock, just as planned. But where was Jason? He was cutting things a bit close.

She stood in a corner of the dining room where she could see the front door and bit her lip. Glancing beseechingly at Stacy, she shrugged her shoulders and raised her hands. Her friend stepped close to her and whispered, "Maybe you should call him?"

Kristi shook her head. They weren't even married yet... she didn't want to start nagging him now! Still, the men were cooking and carving, and the mothers were filling the serving dishes. It was almost time to put the food on the table.

She reached into her pocket for her cell phone just as the front door opened. Jason rushed in, glanced around, and strode quickly to Kristi.

"I'm so sorry," he said, grabbing her free hand and kissing her cheek. "I should've been here an hour ago."

She beamed at him, pulling her hand out of her pocket— without the phone. "You're here now." She returned his kiss. "I wasn't the least bit worried," she lied. No need to admit she'd been about to call him. He was here. All was right with her world.

"What can I help with?" he asked.

"Go wash up," she said, "then you can help Mark finish carving the turkey."

A very few minutes later, the table groaned under the weight of the feast and everyone took their places around the dining table. The turkey had been a crisp, brown thing of beauty, and everyone but Jason had oohed and aahed over it before Mark had done a masterful job of carving. Soon serving dishes were being passed around and everyone was loading their plates with their favorite delicacies.

"Kristi, this is a fabulous meal," Mark said. He'd sampled most of the dishes and there wasn't a spare inch of his plate uncovered. "You've outdone yourself."

Kristi added a dollop of cranberry sauce to her plate, but shook her head. "Not me. This was totally a group effort. If it was up to just me, we'd be eating at Rizzoli's or the Inn."

Everyone laughed.

"I doubt that," said Mamie. "She had the menu all set when Beth and I arrived, and she scheduled everything like a general. The rest of us were just her foot soldiers."

Jason ate a bite of turkey, then lifted his glass of tea. "Well, here's to the cooks, every last one of you. Teamwork created a delicious meal."

"Hear, hear," everyone echoed and toasted themselves and the meal with iced tea.

For several minutes the only sounds in the dining room were the clink of cutlery on plates and the happy sighs of contented diners. Then a loud *MEEOOOWWWW* sounded, and Kristi jumped to her feet.

"Oh! I forgot the cats!"

She'd closed them in her bedroom that morning to keep them out from under foot while the manic food preparation had been going on in the kitchen. A reasonable safety precaution for both felines and humans, but she should have released them before now.

When she opened the bedroom door, both cats marched out without a glance in her direction, tails high and twitching like standards on a battlefield. They paced, Stitches first closely followed by Between, to the kitchen where they deigned to bat at their food bowls.

Stacy approached, working hard to smother a laugh, and at Kristi's nod of approval, scraped a few bites of turkey and gravy into each cat's bowl.

Stitches and Between sniffed the offering, then settled down to their own Thanksgiving feast.

Kristi and Stacy returned to the table and their own meals.

"I knew I was forgetting something," Kristi said with a wry smile. "Now I know what it was."

Jason chuckled, and soon everyone else joined him, though they did it quietly. After all, no one wanted to wound the cats' dignity even further.

Kristi hid a happy sigh behind her napkin. Even with murder consuming Jason's time and thoughts, Thanksgiving was a success!

Now, if only Saturday would turn out as well!

24

THANKSGIVING EVENING

Jason marveled at how smoothly everyone worked together after the big meal. He hadn't been there for the preparation, had simply enjoyed the resulting feast. Sure, he'd heard Kristi's comments about it being a team effort, but he'd assumed she was just being polite. But now, he was seeing the team in action.

Everyone pitched in to put Kristi's home to rights. Some packaged food— including generous portions to send home with Stacy and Mark— and stored the containers in one of the two refrigerators. Some rinsed dishes and loaded the dishwasher, and others bundled the tablecloth and cloth napkins off to the laundry room. Once the table was bare, Mark helped Jason remove the leaves and store them in a closet... ready for the next big feast.

Stacy and Mark gathered up their assigned leftovers and said their goodbyes.

"Thank you so much for inviting us," Stacy said, kissing Kristi on the cheek.

"Of course," Kristi said with a smile. "You know you're welcome any time. Besides, you two certainly worked hard enough for your supper."

"Nice to have met you all," Mark said to Ed and Beth, Reggie and Mamie.

"And you," Ed said for all of them. "Now we'll recognize some faces at the wedding!"

When the front door closed, the remaining six collapsed in the living room.

"I don't know about the rest of you," Jason said, "but I feel a food-induced nap coming on."

Groans of agreement sounded around the room. Reggie leaned back in Jason's big recliner and sighed. "I think I've got the best seat in the house."

Jason, sitting in the corner of the couch with Kristi snuggled up against him, disagreed. "I don't think so," he whispered, but quietly, for Kristi's ears only.

They turned on the television and chose an old, black and white movie, keeping the sound low so everyone could relax and watch, nap, or simply veg out for a while.

Around what would normally have been dinner time, the group roused.

"Anyone hungry?" Kristi asked. "We can have turkey sandwiches or just graze on leftovers."

"Definitely not ready for food yet," Beth said, "but you know what I am interested in?" Kristi raised her eyebrows, and her mom continued, "I'd like a tour of your shop. We've been so busy since we arrived that we haven't had a chance to see it."

Mamie sat up a little straighter. "Oh, yes! That's a great idea. I'd like to see it too."

"Of course I want to see my daughter's business," Ed said quickly. "What about you, Reggie? Want to come?"

Reggie considered. "Well, I'm not much on fabric stores, but sure. Why not?" He gave Kristi a questioning glance. "It's closed, right?"

Kristi laughed. "Yes. The store is closed, and I'd love to give you all a tour. Shall we go now?"

They managed to squeeze everyone into Kristi's Subaru and Jason's Trail Blazer and drove to the shop. Parking in the small, gravel lot behind the store, Kristi unlocked the back door.

"Of course," she said, "you're coming in the wrong way. Customers enter through the front door." She ushered everyone in and turned on the lights. "This is the kitchen / break room. Come on through to the main sales floor."

She led the way, turning on lights as she went. Standing beside the cutting table, she twirled, gesturing around herself. "Welcome to *Delectable Mountain Quilting.*"

"Oh, Kristi," her mom said, "it's beautiful!" Turning to Mamie, Beth said, "Just look at these fabrics! The colors. The way she's displayed them."

"Gorgeous," Mamie said, running her fingers over a bolt of colorful batik fabric. "Kristi, this is so inviting. I'm not even a quilter and I'm itching to buy fabric!"

Reggie placed a hand on his wife's shoulder. "Easy there. The last thing you need is another project to cart home."

Mamie laughed. "True enough." She turned to Kristi. "But if it affects me this way, I imagine quilters who walk through that door rarely leave empty handed."

Kristi smiled. "I'm glad you like it. And yes, the business is doing quite well."

Ed placed an arm around Kristi's shoulders. "I always knew there was a business woman hiding inside you." He gave her a squeeze. "This just proves it. We're so very proud of you, sweetheart."

Jason, who had been leaning against the door frame between the sales floor and the break room, smiled. He was proud of Kristi too, and thrilled that both sets of parents were being so appreciative of her hard work. He had no need to join in the discussion, but was content to observe and take note of what the others said. Especially his dad. Jason knew Reggie could come off as remote and guarded, so he wanted to store up the nice comments Reggie made so Jason could remind Kristi of them later.

And, he reminded himself, he needed to do that for anything positive Reggie said about himself as well. Good to remember that his dad wasn't finding fault with him. At least, not all the time.

Feeling content, Jason was surprised when his cell phone rang. Pulling it out of his pocket, he checked the display. Dispatch.

"Sheriff Reynolds," he said, stepping into the break room so he wouldn't disturb the others.

"This is Anita, Sheriff," a female voice said. Clara was off for the holiday. Anita was the back-up dispatcher. "A Steve Gibbs called for you. He says he has urgent information regarding the murders. He'd like you to call as soon as possible."

Jason smothered a sigh, pulled out his little notebook, and took down the phone numbers Anita provided.

"Thanks, Anita. I'll take care of it." Jason clicked off and called Gibbs. A few minutes later, he strode into the main part of the shop.

"Sorry, everyone, but I've got to go back to work. Mom. Dad. Do you want me to take you back to Kristi's or to the Inn? I can drop you either place on my way."

Reggie and Mamie glanced at each other, then turned to Kristi. "It's been a lovely day, Kristi, but I think Mamie and I will head back to the Inn now. Is that all right?"

"Of course," Kristi said, giving each of them a kiss. Turning to Jason, she said, "Be careful. Call if there's anything I can do."

"Always." He kissed her cheek. "Take care of your folks. I'll see you tomorrow." And with that he ushered his parents out to his Trail Blazer.

A short time later, Jason knocked on Eula Gibbs front door. When the older woman answered, he touched the brim of his Stetson and said, "Eula. I believe Steve is expecting me."

"Yes," she said. "Thank you for coming, Sheriff. He's been antsy all day. I'm hoping whatever it is he needs to talk to you about will give him some peace."

Jason followed her down a hall and into what appeared to be her sewing room. Steve Gibbs sat in a swivel chair beside a sewing machine. Another chair waited opposite him.

"You two can talk privately in here," Eula said. "I'll close the door. The rest of the family is in the dining room, if you need anything."

"Thank you, Eula," Jason said, removing his Stetson and his shearling coat and moving to the second chair. "I'm sure we'll be fine."

The moment the door closed, Jason sat, looked directly in the man's eyes, and said, "Okay, Steve. Let's hear it."

FRIDAY MORNING

After a good night's sleep, Kristi awoke rested and relaxed... and thrilled that Thanksgiving was in the past! She missed sharing her bed with Jason, but both sets of parents would be leaving soon, and life would get back to normal.

Then she remembered.

She and Jason were getting married tomorrow!

Sitting straight up in bed, her heart racing and her palms sweating, she inhaled deep breaths trying to decide if she was terrified or thrilled. The combination of opposite emotions definitely didn't sit well with her. While she gasped and wheezed and tried — largely unsuccessfully— to bring her emotions under control, Stitches and Between jumped lightly onto the bed.

The two cats simply sat and stared at her for a moment. Then Stitches rubbed against her right arm, purring like a NASCAR engine, while Between stepped into her lap, kneaded her thighs for a moment, then turned circles until he found the perfect angle and curled into a warm, purring weight. Almost as if he was grounding her, holding her firmly on the earth.

Kristi relaxed and smiled. Who could panic in the face of such love and acceptance?

"Thank you, kitty-kids," she murmured, stroking each of her cats. "You know who else loves and accepts me? Jason. That's who. That's why I'm not the least bit worried about marrying him. I love him. He loves me. Everything will be fine."

And it would be. It wasn't Jason she was panicking about, it was the ceremony. And that would be fine as well. Even if everything went wrong, she'd still marry Jason, and their friends would still be their friends.

Her heart rate calmed and her breathing normalized. That rested and relaxed feeling returned and she knew whatever the day held, she'd handle it.

"Okay, kitty-kids. Crisis averted." She shooed them aside, flipped the covers back, and scooted to the edge of the bed. "Let's get dressed and go fix breakfast."

Both cats alerted to their favorite word: *breakfast*. The hopped off the bed and pranced to the bathroom. They knew her morning routine. First the bathroom, then the closet, then the wonderful kitchen where food would miraculously appear in their bowls.

Kristi laughed at them, but followed their suggestion and got her day underway. She rarely wore cosmetics, and today was no exception, but she brushed her shoulder-length blonde hair and pulled it into a high ponytail. Turning to her closet, she chose to dress casually in jeans and an over-sized flannel shirt.

When her parents emerged from the guest room, Kristi had breakfast well under way. Scrambled eggs, crisp bacon, toast and jelly were almost ready to be scooped onto plates and carried to the table.

"I was going to volunteer to fix breakfast," Ed said. "Guess I'll have to get up a little earlier to pull that off."

"Appreciate the thought," Kristi said as she plated the food. "You can put your name in for tomorrow, if you want."

Beth nodded. "Good idea. Kristi shouldn't be taking care of us on her wedding morning."

"Then it's settled," Ed said, rubbing his hands together in anticipation. "Tomorrow I'm the cook for breakfast."

"Great. Grab the plates and the jelly and head to the table," Kristi said. "I'll bring the coffee pot and some mugs."

Beth glanced at the cats, sitting quietly beside their bowls. "Have the cats eaten?"

"Definitely," Kristi said with a smile. "You wouldn't be able to move without them trying to wind around your ankles if they hadn't. Don't let them pull the *starving kitty* act on you."

Once everyone was seated, Kristi poured mugs of coffee for each of them, and they settled down to eat.

"What's on the agenda for today?" Ed asked.

"Stacy's coming over this morning and bringing her lists." Kristi almost rolled her eyes, but managed to stop herself just in time.

"Lists?" asked Beth.

Kristi nodded, sipped her coffee, and said, "She's got the wedding planned out to the minute. She'll let us know who's doing what and when they're doing it." She shook her head. "Stace is a great organizer; I'm lucky to have her on my side."

"I swear," Beth said, "that girl might as well move in with you. She's been here every day since we arrived."

"Not that that's a bad thing," Ed added quickly.

"Definitely not," Kristi said. "Besides, Mark would miss her if she didn't come home every night."

All three smiled and they finished their breakfast in silence. They'd just cleaned up the kitchen when the doorbell rang.

"I'll get it," Ed said, hanging his dishtowel on the oven door.

A moment later, Kristi heard him greet Stacy. She and Beth hurried to the living room to join them.

Stacy hugged Kristi. "Are you ready for the big day?"

The butterflies returned in full force as Kristi pulled away from her friend, but she managed a bright smile. "Of course. Have you got all our plans in place?"

Stacy grinned. "You bet! Let's get comfortable and I'll tell you everything."

Ed, looking a little nervous, excused himself. "I've got some reading to do," he said and escaped to his bedroom.

"Men!" Beth shook her head, but smiled. "He'd rather be fishing than listening to details about a wedding."

The three women settled around the coffee table and Stacy pulled out her planner.

"Now, here's what we know." She launched into a detailed description of the wedding venue at the *Garnet Gateway Inn* as well as the plans for the reception after the ceremony.

Kristi closed her eyes, picturing it. "That sounds wonderful, Stacy. Thank you for arranging everything."

Stacy waved away the thanks. "No problem! Now, do you want to have a rehearsal this evening? I can arrange it, if you do."

Kristi blinked. She hadn't even thought about rehearsing. "No. I don't think so. I mean, it's not that complicated a ceremony. We don't have lots of attendants or special music or anything like that."

Beth raised her hand, then, laughing at herself, put it down again. "Speaking of the ceremony, who's officiating?"

Kristi paled. "I knew I forgot something," she muttered.

Stacy laughed. "Fortunately, I didn't." She reached over and patted Kristi's knee. "I talked to Jason about that earlier in the week. We decided that since neither of you are particularly religious, you'd be better off with a civil ceremony. And since Jason is the sheriff, Judge Evers said he'd be delighted to officiate."

Kristi sighed in relief. How could she have forgotten that *someone* had to officiate? "Thank you, Stacy. You're a live saver... and so is the judge!"

"Don't worry," Stacy said. "Everything's under control. All you have to do is show up!"

Beth and Kristi listened and nodded their approval as Stacy detailed the rest of the plans. Eula's gardening group had Kristi's bouquet and other flowers all ready for the big day. DeAnna's brother-in-law, Owen Waters, would arrive early to take photos of the room before the ceremony, and Kristi's staff would have the quilt they'd been working on displayed for all of the guests to admire.

"They're making you a quilt?" Beth asked.

"They are," Kristi said, her eyes shining with happiness. "A Double Wedding Ring, and the last time I saw it, it was absolutely gorgeous!"

"You must have amazing employees, Kristi," Beth said. "I'm looking forward to meeting them."

"I do," Kristi agreed. "I definitely do."

"Well," Stacy said, "I happen to know that Kristi's staff think they have the best employer around." She met Kristi's gaze and nodded. "They love you, Kristi, as evidenced by all their help with the wedding in addition to making a quilt for you and Jason. They didn't have to step up, you know."

"I do know," Kristi said, nodding, "and I'm humbled by their support." She reached for Stacy's hand. "And for yours. You're the best, Stacy."

"I'm your friend," Stacy said, tears sparkling in her eyes, "and I love you too." She squeezed Kristi's hand, then sat up a little straighter. "I think that does it. You're going to have a beautiful wedding!"

She beamed at Kristi and Beth. "See you two at Rizzoli's tonight for the rehearsal dinner."

Kristi laughed. "Is it still a rehearsal dinner if we're not doing a rehearsal?"

"Who cares?" asked Stacy. "It's dinner at Rizzoli's. That's a celebration all by itself!"

FRIDAY AFTERNOON

Jason and his deputies were having a very busy day. They'd begun the morning by checking out the story Steve Gibbs had told Jason last night.

Steve claimed that Jerry Wanamaker had died because of a young girl. A girl barely into her teens that Jerry had sold drugs to, and who had subsequently died.

"That doesn't wash, Gibbs," Jason had said. "We already did a search for drug-related deaths prior to Wanamaker's death. We didn't find any. Especially not a young teen female."

Gibbs had thrown his hands in the air and paced his grandmother's sewing room. "That's because Amber's death wouldn't have been listed as drug-related. The coroner ruled it an accident. Misadventure or some such fancy term. But her family laid it at Jerry's door. He sold her drugs. She got hooked. Her family intervened and made sure she couldn't get her fix. She got hold of her father's revolver and offed herself. End of story."

Jason heard him out, nodded, and said, "What's this girl's name? Her full name, Amber isn't enough."

"Amber Davidson."

Jason wrote the name in his notebook. "I'll check it out. Now, I get the possible connection to Wanamaker. What makes you think this has anything to do with Carrick and Jennings?"

"It's the carousel," Gibbs said. "Everyone knew it was Amber's favorite place. She loved those stupid fake horses. Thought the music and lights were magical. When Jerry's body turned up there, we knew it was about Amber. Billy and Tommie and me, we hightailed it out of here as soon as we heard about Jerry. Went to Helena and haven't been back. Until now." He dropped into the swivel chair by the sewing machine and stared at his hands. "Shouldn't have come back even now, but Gran wanted to see me. So did Billy and Tommie's folks."

He raised his head and met Jason's eyes, his own filled with grief, and more than a little fear. "Course, if we'd stayed in Helena, Billy'd still be alive."

Jason didn't comment on that, instead he asked, "What did Carrick and Jennings have to do with Amber's death? Or you and Atwood?"

Gibbs closed his eyes and leaned back in his grandmother's chair. "Not a damn thing. We were all good buddies in high school, and Billy and Tommie and me ragged on Jerry, trying to get him to let us in on his little business, but he wouldn't take us on. Said his distributors didn't want a bunch of know-nothings like us working for them."

"What about Carrick?"

"Ray never even asked to be included. He'd met Denise and was walking the straight and narrow. Ray had absolutely nothing to do with selling drugs. He and Denise were busy making a life together. A good life. He didn't want anything to do with any of us or our get rich quick schemes."

"And yet," Jason said, "he was the first of you to die."

———

THAT WAS LAST NIGHT.

This morning, Jason and his deputies had been busy verifying Gibbs' story. His account of Amber's death held. The coroner's ruling had been reasonable. She'd had no drugs in her system and her parents had failed to mention her addiction or the depression she'd been dealing with after her forced withdrawal.

If the addiction and withdrawal had actually happened.

Eric Lawson had discovered that the mother, Cissy Davidson, had committed suicide a year to the day after Amber's death.

That left the father, Henry, and a younger brother, Noah.

Two men. Two wounds in each victim. Two separate knives used.

Jason was considering how to approach the Davidsons when Eula Gibbs called in a panic. Clara put the call through to Jason immediately.

"Sheriff," Eula cried. "I don't know what to do. A man and a teenage boy came by and grabbed Steve right out of our back-yard. I don't know what he told you last night, but I know my grandson is scared, and now these men…" She sobbed to a stop. Took a breath and tried again. "What should I do, Sheriff?"

"You've done it, Eula," Jason said, his voice calm and firm. "We'll take it from here."

Ending the call, Jason turned to his deputies. "Let's move!"

"Where to, Sheriff?" asked Eric Lawson.

"The carousel," he said as he pulled on his shearling coat. "We may have a murder in progress. Let's hope it's only attempted at this point." He paused as he reached the door and turned to Clara. "Call emergency services. Have an ambulance meet us at Riverside Park."

Jason and Eric Lawson climbed into Jason's Trail Blazer, while Evan Knott rode with Janet. Both vehicles used their lights and sirens as they sped to the carousel. Pulling into the empty parking area, the four of them jumped from their vehicles and ran to the carousel.

What they saw, stopped them in their tracks. Steve Gibbs, bound and gagged, sagged on the bench where Carrick, and later Jennings, had died. A grizzled man and a boy, around fifteen, stood over him with knives in their hands.

Jason gestured to his deputies and they spread out, drawing their guns.

"Henry Davidson," Jason called. "You don't want to do anything to endanger yourself or young Noah." He waited a beat, letting the afternoon's stillness settle around them all. "Put down the weapons. Henry, think about Noah. Your boy doesn't want to do this."

Henry Davidson didn't so much as glance at Jason. He kept his gaze steady, his knife aimed at Gibbs' chest. The man's hands were steady, but he was disheveled. His jeans and flannel shirt looked like they hadn't been laundered in weeks. His graying hair was overlong and messy, his sunken cheeks stubbled. The boy, Noah, was thin and ragged, his dirty blond hair tousled and his eyes tired and hopeless.

"This is necessary, Sheriff," Henry said, his gaze never leaving his intended victim. "It's justice for my Amber. For Cissy." Tears swam in his eyes, but he blinked them back. "The law failed them. I won't. And I won't let Noah fail them either."

Jason took a step closer. Noted that his deputies were slowly, carefully, tightening the circle as well. "The law never had a chance, Davidson. You withheld information. If you'd told us what really happened to Amber, we would've brought Wanamaker and his associates to justice." He holstered his gun, raised his hands, and stepped up onto the base of the carousel behind the bench where Gibbs was restrained. "Instead, you took the law into your own hands. Look at me, Davison!"

When the man obeyed Jason's command and raised his eyes to Jason, his knife hand wavered. Eric leapt onto the platform and knocked the man to the ground. The knife clattered away and Jason raced to step on it before Davidson had a chance to get control of it again. Eric handcuffed the man.

While Eric grappled with the father, Janet jumped onto the carousel and grabbed the son, forcing him to drop his knife as well. The boy didn't put up much of a fight. It was clear Noah didn't want to be there, but couldn't disobey his father.

"I'm sorry," the boy sobbed. "Dad just went nuts last week, and I… I didn't know how to stop him."

Jason knelt beside Noah. "What set him off? Do you know?"

"He… he took his car in to be worked on. Heard Ray Carrick say something about missing his high school buds… especially one who died. Jerry Wanamaker."

Jason shook his head. "And from a single, nostalgic comment your dad decided Ray and his friends were as guilty as Wanamaker." He straightened to standing. "What a waste."

Janet read both assailants their rights, while Jason released Steve Gibbs. Once the gag was out, Steve asked, "How did you find me? I thought I was a dead man."

Jason pulled him to his feet, and said, "You likely would've been if your grandmother hadn't those two grab you. Eula called it in."

"What now, Sheriff?"

"You go on home, Steve," Jason said, clapping a hand on the younger man's shoulder, "but don't leave town. My deputies will need to speak to you next week. Likely someone from the prosecutor's office will as well."

"Not you, Sheriff?"

Jason grinned. "Not me. I'm getting married tomorrow... and then I'll be on my honeymoon. Don't give my deputies any trouble or I'll have to hunt you down when I get back."

"No, sir. Wouldn't dream of it." He gave Jason a shy grin. "Congratulations, Sheriff."

Jason nodded. "Thanks. Now go thank your grandmother. She's the one who saved your life."

27

FRIDAY EVENING

When Kristi and her parents arrived at *Rizzoli's Fine Italian Restaurant*, they discovered Mark and Stacy, Mamie and Reggie already seated at the table in the private dining room Mama Rizzoli had reserved for them.

Kristi glanced around. "Where's Jason?"

"He's on his way," Mark said quickly. "He was tied up at the station and asked Stacy and I to give his folks a lift."

"I hope everything's okay," Kristi said as she seated herself beside Stacy. "I know he's been concerned about closing this case before we leave town."

"Don't you worry, Kristi," Reggie said, reaching across the table to pat her hand. "His staff will pick up the slack if he hasn't solved it yet."

"That's right," Mamie agreed. "Jason is getting married tomorrow. He won't let anything, even murder, interfere with that."

"Definitely not," Jason said with a laugh. Mama Rizzoli had ushered him into the room just in time to hear his mother's comment. Striding to the table, he kissed Kristi's cheek and settled into the chair beside her. "Looks like I'm late again, but it's the last time. I'm officially off duty until after our honeymoon."

"Did you close the case?" Ed asked.

"Sure did. The killers are locked up and Garnet Gateway can return to its normal winter slumbers."

"Congratulations," Mark said, "and good job, Sheriff."

"Yes," said Kristi, "and I want to hear all about it, but for right now, let's study our menus and decide what to order before Mama Rizzoli comes back."

They quietly scanned their menus for a moment. The out-of-towners with more diligence than the four who lived in Garnet Gateway and ate at Rizzoli's fairly frequently.

Mamie was the first to look up. "Everything looks so good," she said. "What do you recommend?"

"You can't go wrong with anything on this menu," Stacy said confidently. "We all have our favorites, and tend to order the same thing all the time, but I've never had a disappointing meal here."

"That's true," Kristi added. "Remember the lasagna we had earlier this week? That was a take-out dish from here... and my personal favorite. Though I also love their shrimp Alfredo."

"I almost always order spaghetti and meatballs," Jason said. "Kristi teases me about not being very adventurous, but I say why mess with perfection?"

Everyone was laughing as Mama Rizzoli appeared at their table. "Good," the plump, gray haired woman said with a smile. "Happy customers are the best customers." She patted Kristi's cheek before resting a hand on Jason's shoulder. "And who wouldn't be happy when you're celebrating these two wonderful people?"

She glanced between the four parents. "Did you know that Jason proposed to Kristi right here in our restaurant?" She lowered her voice to a stage whisper. "It was very romantic." She straightened to her full, and not very imposing, height and pulled out her order pad. "We're very proud of our Sheriff and his beautiful bride, but right now... what can I bring you for dinner?"

Ordering was a bit hectic and confused, since the parents kept changing their minds as they heard what the locals were choosing, but Mama was good-natured about it and eventually decisions were made. A remarkably short time later, Mama reappeared carrying two folding serving stands and followed by two dark-haired teenage boys carrying large trays loaded with their meals. After the boys deposited the trays on the stands, Mama nodded and the young men returned to the kitchen, passing a young woman at the door to the private dining room. She carried a serving stand in one hand and a tray of wine bottles and stemmed glasses on the other. When all was in place, Mama distributed the plates while the young woman served the wine.

"Chicken parmigiana for the mother of the bride," Mama said, placing a steaming plate in front of Beth.

"And spaghetti marinara for her father."

Moving back to the tray, she picked up a plate and turned to Mamie. "For the mother of the groom, our special: Chicken Marsala."

"And for our sheriff's father, spaghetti and meatballs." She smiled and added, "Like father, like son!"

Turning her attention to Stacy, she placed a bountiful plate of pasta on the table. "Fettuccine Alfredo for you, my dear. And for your husband, spaghetti with meat sauce."

Grinning with delight, she turned to Kristi and Jason. "I've saved the best for last! For our beautiful bride, her favorite, our classic lasagna. And for her handsome groom, our brave sheriff, his favorite, spaghetti and meatballs!"

Mama clapped her hands and beamed. "Enjoy!" Then she and her assistant sailed from the room.

"Oh, my goodness," cried Beth. "This all looks and smells amazing! I can't wait to taste it."

"No need to wait," called Jason. "Dig in!"

For a few minutes, all conversation ceased as everyone enjoyed their meals. When appetites had been sated, the diners sat back, one by one, and turned their attention to Jason.

His dad spoke first. "I'm sure I'm not the only one who's curious. How did you case turn out?"

Jason thought for a moment, then gave his audience the condensed version of the murder investigation, leaving out names and gory details.

"Was Eula's information helpful?" Kristi asked.

Jason nodded. "In fact, her grandson was the reason we were able to solve it. You should ask her about it sometime. I'm pretty sure Eula is now her grandson's personal heroine."

"And the two men you arrested," Mark said. "You said one was still a teen?"

Jason's expression became shadowed. "Yes, and I think that's a tragedy. I don't think that youngster wanted to participate, but was bullied into it by his father." He sighed. "I'm hoping my chief deputy can talk our prosecutor into going easy on the boy." He glanced at his father. "But that's out of my jurisdiction. We lawmen gather evidence and make arrests. It's up to the courts to dispense judgment."

Reggie nodded. "That's true, but I'm glad to hear your chief deputy will put in a good word for the boy. We do have an obligation to make our thoughts known. After all, they're informed opinions."

And with that, conversation turned to happier matters. Like tomorrow's wedding!

Mark sipped his chianti then leaned forward to meet Jason's gaze. "So, Reynolds, where are you taking Kristi for your honeymoon?"

Jason raised an eyebrow and gave Mark what Kristi always thought of as his *cop's stare*. "None of your business, Robards."

Mark laughed and raised his hands in mock surrender. "Don't shoot, Sheriff. I was just asking!"

"Well, don't," Jason said, glaring at his friend. He turned to Kristi, his gaze softening. "It's a surprise." He picked up her hand and kissed it. "I think you're going to love it."

"I'm sure I will," she said quietly. She gazed into his eyes and prayed he could see her fervent love. "You're all I need."

28

THE WEDDING

Jason stared at himself in the full length mirror in his parents' room at the Garnet Gateway Inn. This was his wedding day... and it had been the longest morning of his life; he was a man of action, and there'd been nothing for him to do.

He couldn't go over to Kristi's— grooms weren't supposed to see brides before the wedding.

He couldn't go in to the station— he was logged out for his wedding and honeymoon.

He couldn't even walk around the town he was bound to serve and protect. He'd tried, but every other person he'd passed had wanted to know why he wasn't busy getting ready for his wedding?

They might be having a small ceremony, but it seemed every single citizen of Garnet Gateway knew this was his wedding day.

Finally, he'd given up, packed his bag for the honeymoon, grabbed his garment bag, and driven to the Inn to impose on his folks.

Not they thought it was an imposition. Reggie and Mamie were delighted to find him knocking on their door. After a light room-service lunch of tomato soup and grilled cheese sandwiches, Mamie had excused herself. She'd dressed earlier in a dark blue wool suit dress that looked stunning with her snowy hair.

She placed a hand on her son's cheek as she was leaving. "I've enjoyed our time together this morning, Jason. I'm glad you came, but now you need a bit of time with your father to get ready. I'll head up to the conference room to see if I can help with the decorating." She glanced at her husband. "See you two there."

"I guess that was our hint," Reggie said, slapping his knees and preparing to stand. "Time for us to get ready. What are you wearing to this shindig?"

Jason unzipped his garment bag and showed his dad the suit he'd bought just for this occasion. "What about you?"

"Your mother made me spring for a traditional black suit." Reggie strode to the closet and pulled it out. Glancing between the two garments, he said, "I like yours better."

Jason laughed. "Well, that's probably as it should be. You're not the one getting married."

The two men carried on a light banter as they dressed, and now Jason stared at himself in the room's full length mirror. He looked good. The charcoal gray suit was cut in the western style and suited him to a T. Combined with his favorite string tie with its silver star slider and his best black cowboy boots, he felt ready for anything. All he needed was his black Stetson, but that was best left with his luggage. He didn't need his hat for the ceremony.

When both men were ready, they headed to the conference room where Jason greeted Judge Evers and joined Mark Robards, who would be standing with him through the ceremony.

"You've got the rings?" he asked Mark.

His friend patted his pocket. "Right here. Everything's set, Jason. You don't have to worry about a thing. Just make your vows."

Jason nodded and turned to watch for Kristi.

———

KRISTI HAD ENJOYED a leisurely breakfast with her parents before indulging in some serious snuggling with her kitty-kids. After all, once she left the house today, she wouldn't see Stitches or Between for more than a week. She knew Stacy would take good care of them, but still… she'd miss the cats who had been her constant companions for the last several years. She hoped they wouldn't be too annoyed with her for the long absence.

She closed her eyes, wondering what Jason had planned for their honeymoon. He hadn't dropped a single hint. Knowing how he loved the mountains, she'd packed for a winter adventure. If he surprised her with a tropical getaway, he'd have to spring for a whole new wardrobe. She grinned mischievously as the thought struck that if an island getaway was private enough, she might not need a wardrobe at all!

But that was just silly. Neither of them was wealthy enough to pull that kind of thing off. But still, a girl could dream.

And right now, this girl's dream was simply to marry Jason and then not have to share him with all of Garnet County for a few days!

Wherever he planned to take her, they'd be alone and that was all that mattered.

At lunch time, Beth fixed turkey sandwiches with a side of cranberry sauce, but Kristi wasn't sure she could eat. The butterflies in her tummy were flying wild loop-de-loops.

Beth patted her hand. "Just take a bite. You don't have to eat the whole thing."

To please her mother, Kristi took a nibble… and found her appetite after all.

The doorbell rang as they were rinsing the dishes.

"That'll be Stacy," Kristi announced.

"Hey there, Bride! Let's grab your things and head to the Inn."

"But I'm not dressed," Kristi exclaimed, panic setting the butterflies into motion once more.

Stacy rolled her eyes. "I can see that! Let's go anyway. I've arranged for a dressing room at the Inn. We don't want you to arrive with your hem all messy from walking in from the parking lot! Are you packed?"

"Sure…"

"Well, let's get this show on the road! Give your dad your car keys. Your folks can follow us over, then your mom and I can help you get ready while your dad visits with Mark."

Stacy chivvied the bride into her car after making sure Kristi had everything she'd need… both for the wedding ceremony and the honeymoon. Beth and Ed had decided to get dressed at home, but promised to join Stacy and Kristi within the hour.

Soon Kristi found herself ensconced in a lovely dressing room next to the conference room that would serve as her wedding chapel. She managed a quick glance inside, but Stacy insisted she keep moving.

"Don't worry. Your friends are doing a wonderful job decorating. Your job is to get into that dress and let me help with your hair and make-up."

By the time Beth arrived, Kristi was standing in front of a full length mirror wearing her wedding dress.

"Oh, Kristi," her mother breathed. "You look beautiful. And that dress! It's… perfect."

And it was. The a-line gown flowed from a fitted bodice, gradually flaring from waist to floor with graceful bishop's sleeves ending in wide cuffs fastened with pearl buttons.

Beth walked around her daughter. "You told me it was gold, but this isn't just gold, it's… perfect." The color brought out the highlights in Kristi's hair, but it wasn't just a single shade of gold. The color flowed from the palest of creamy yellow at the bateau neckline to the deepest shade of burnished gold at the hem.

"She's a vision, isn't she?" Stacy asked, her eyes sparkling with happy tears. "But we're not finished. Come here, Kristi. Have a seat and let me work on your hair."

Grinning at her mother and best friend's approval of her dress, Kristi moved to the dressing table and surrendered to their ministrations for her hair and cosmetics.

When all was ready, Stacy slipped out to join Mark and Jason at the front of the room with the judge. Beth also slipped out, but she went in search of Kristi's father. Once Ed joined his daughter, Beth took her seat in the front row of guests.

Everyone who'd been invited was in attendance. *Delectable Mountain Quilting* was closed for the day, so all of Kristi's staff were there along with husbands and boyfriends. Deputy Roger Jepperson was holding down the fort at the sheriff's department while Janet Millson and the rest of Jason's crew were seated among the guests.

As soon as Stacy saw Kristi and her dad appear in the doorway, she signaled the Inn's audio tech and a recording of Pachelbel's "Canon in D Major" began to play. Jason came to attention, his gaze glued to the vision in gold who was his beautiful bride. The guests rose to watch as Ed escorted his daughter to her groom.

But Kristi and Jason had eyes only for each other. As though no one else existed in their universe.

EPILOGUE

Kristi relaxed in the passenger seat of Jason's Trail Blazer, her head supported on the padded neck rest, her gaze on her new husband.

Husband.

Jason was once again her husband and she was his wife.

She smiled. The wedding had been perfect! Her friends had decorated the conference room with more flowers than she would've guessed could possibly be in bloom in late November in Montana. Eula had proudly presented Kristi with a small bouquet of pale yellow roses and white baby's breath. They'd also relented about Kristi not seeing the quilt until after her honeymoon. Instead, they'd set up a quilt stand to one side of the windows and displayed the priceless gift... a king-size Double Wedding Ring quilt. A quilt made by those same friends with love just for Kristi and Jason.

And then there was the room itself! Stacy had outdone herself in finding a room with such a glorious view of the Absaroka Mountains.

It was so much better than what Kristi had originally planned: a simple ceremony in her living room with only her parents and Mark and Stacy in attendance.

Celebrating with their friends had been a delight.

As for the ceremony itself… perfection! Judge Evers wasn't a man given to flowery speeches. He'd said what needed to be said, allowed them to speak their vows to each other, and pronounced them husband and wife. Short and to the point. Exactly what Kristi had hoped for.

"It was a wonderful wedding," Jason said, glancing at her and smiling. "Everyone did a great job pulling it together."

"They did, didn't they."

"And the Inn really came through, too. The food was amazing."

Kristi nodded. "I really liked the little petit fours. So much better than a big wedding cake… and nothing to have to cut."

"Your staff did such a beautiful job on that quilt. My mom was absolutely blown away by it. What do you call that pattern?"

"It's a Double Wedding Ring," she said dreamily. "A traditional pattern for a new marriage." She was a lucky woman. Jason couldn't care less about quilts—except as a warm blanket for a bed—or quilting in general, but he supported her love for the craft and genuinely liked her employees and friends.

They rode in silence for a few minutes as Jason drove south into the gathering darkness.

South. Not north to Billings. So they weren't boarding a plane and flying away to the tropics. Kristi grinned. She hadn't really expected that they would. Jason would've planned a honeymoon much closer to home. After all, they only had a little over a week

—they were both expected back to work a week from Monday. Why waste time in airports and crowded into planes?

"You haven't told me where we're going," she said, watching him closely for any clues in his reaction.

"Nope. I haven't."

"Are you going to?"

"Nope. You'll see when we get there."

She frowned, wondering what she could ask next. Finally she asked, "Is it much farther?"

He laughed. "Is that anything like *are we there yet?*"

She punched him lightly on the shoulder. "You're teasing me!"

He turned his gaze on her for a moment and grinned. "I certainly am, and I'm enjoying every minute of it." Eyes back on the road again, he said, "Seriously though, it's not much further. We'll arrive before it's full dark."

She settled back into her seat, content. They must be headed to Yellowstone. That was the only place this road led unless they were driving through the park and out again to someplace like West Yellowstone, and that would take longer than the time frame he'd given.

A Yellowstone honeymoon. She could appreciate that.

But they didn't go to Yellowstone.

Kristi straightened in her seat when Jason turned off the highway before they even reached Gardiner. He drove east toward the 'Sorkees. Where in the world was he taking her?

They reached the foothills, driving into tall timber. As the pines surrounded them, they drove under an entrance arch and up ahead, the drive widened to show a large, lighted lodge.

Jason pulled under a porte cochere and parked. "Welcome to 'Sorkee Retreat," he said, opening his door and grinning hugely.

Kristi sat as if paralyzed, staring that the large log building. It was beautifully proportioned, with lights twinkling from every window. And there were lots of windows.

Jason opened her door and offered her his hand. Neither of them were still wearing their wedding clothes. They'd changed into much more casual attire, jeans and flannel shirts, for the drive. Now Kristi wondered if she was underdressed for such an elegant looking resort.

She took Jason's hand and stepped out of the vehicle. "What is this place?" she whispered.

Jason put his arm around her and led her to the entrance. "They bill it as a luxury ranch resort." He stopped and gazed into her eyes. "I've booked us a private cabin. Meals are included and will be delivered to our door. We don't have to see anyone for the whole week if we don't want to."

"It sounds heavenly," she murmured.

He kissed her, then led her forward again. "Let's check in. I want to be alone with you."

The cabin was truly a sanctuary in the trees. There wasn't another building in sight. Inside the log cabin offered a comfortable living area with a fire already crackling in the river rock fireplace. A fully stocked kitchen, in case they needed a snack between the delivered meals. And a bedroom right out of a romance novel!

The king-size rustic aspen log bed was topped with a beautifully crafted log cabin quilt done in blues and reds and golds. The matching bedside tables and vanity were also made of aspen logs. The en suite bath featured double sinks, a roomy shower, and a soaking tub designed to accommodate two.

"Oh, Jason!" Kristi said as she stroked the beautiful quilt. "This is exactly the right honeymoon for us."

He moved behind her and embraced her. Nuzzling her neck, he said, "I thought you'd like it."

She turned in his arms and kissed him. Soundly and deeply. "I do."

He smiled and nipped her bottom lip. "My favorite words."

She gazed into his eyes. "I love you, Jason. I always have, and I always will."

He nodded. "As I do you, Kristi. Now and forever."

He picked her up and laid her on the bed. "Shall we truly begin our marriage?"

She grinned. "Let's. Immediately!"

Joining her on the bed, he gazed at her with so much love that Kristi thought her heart might just overflow.

She was married— again!— to the man of dreams. He loved her and she loved him, and they had a lifetime together to explore that love.

Starting right now, in a private cabin deep in the tall timber of the foothills of the Absarokas. Her new favorite place on earth!

ALSO BY DEBBIE MUMFORD

Kristi Lundrigan Mysteries:

- DELECTABLE MOUNTAIN QUILTING (NOVEL)
- IN A PICKLE (NOVEL)
- DOUBLE WEDDING RING (NOVEL)
- FOOL'S PUZZLE (SHORT STORY)
- WILDFIRE! (SHORT STORY)
- CHRISTMAS STAR (SHORT STORY)
- WISH FULFILLMENT (A SHERIFF REYNOLDS SHORT STORY)

Gus and Ghost Short Story Series:

- SEVENTH
- SEVENTH: FIRST FRUITS
- DEATH OF AN ALCHEMIST (UNCOLLECTED ANTHOLOGY)
- SEVENTH: THE SAMHAIN DILEMMA
- DARK OF THE MOON (UNCOLLECTED ANTHOLOGY)
- FLIGHT PLAN (UNCOLLECTED ANTHOLOGY)
- MIDSUMMER NIGHT (UNCOLLECTED ANTHOLOGY)

Logans of Lastalrig Series:

- HER HIGHLAND LAIRD (NOVELLA)
- HER HIGHLAND YULE (SHORT STORY)
- WISE WOMAN (SHORT STORY)

Red's Series:

- RED'S MAGICK (SHORT STORY COLLECTION)
- SEEING RED (SHORT STORY)

Signs of the Prophecy Novels:

- Youngest
- Seeker
- Chosen (Coming Soon!)

Sorcha's Children Series:

- Sorcha's Children (Omnibus Edition)
- Sorcha's Heart (Novella)
- Dragons' Choice (Novel)
- Dragons' Flight (Novel)
- Dragons' Desire (Novel)
- Dragons' Destiny (Novel)

Supernatural Yellowstone Short Story Series:

- Reality Bites
- The Cat Lady of Yellowstone

Uncollected Anthology Short Stories:

- Death of an Alchemist (UA Alchemy)
- The Wedding Cake (UA Magical Arts)
- Dark of the Moon (UA Paranormal Pirates)
- In the Banyan Copse (UA Unexpected Histories)
- Old One (UA Magical Quests)
- Have Hoard, Will Seek (UA A Diversity of Dragons)
- Flight Plan (UA Mystical Maps)
- Disappeared! (UA Were-Creatures & Conundrums)
- Midsummer Night (UA Summer Solstice)

Universal Star League Short Story Series:

- Voyages Into The Black (Collection)
- The Warbirds of Absaroka
- Awakening the Warrior
- Incident on the Odyssey
- The Queen's Captive
- The Lost Colony

- FREIGHTER FAMILIES IN SPACE

Witchling Short Story Series:

- WITCHLING
- THE SOLITARY SORCERESS
- TO PROTECT A PRINCESS

Stand Alone Novels:

- SECOND SIGHT

Historical Fiction:

- HER HIGHLAND LAIRD (NOVELLA)
- HER HIGHLAND YULE
- INCIDENT ON THE HIGH LINE
- MISS BAINBRIDGE'S SUMMER ADVENTURE
- MISS BAINBRIDGE'S CHRISTMAS PARTY
- SISTERS IN SUFFRAGE
- THE TRAIL WHERE WE CRIED
- THE WHITE DRAGON AND THE RED

Short Story Collections:

- LOVE IN A FLASH
- TALES OF BYGONE DAYS
- TALES OF LOVE & MAGICK
- TALES OF THE UNEXPECTED
- TALES OF TOMORROW
- TALES OF DISASTROUS DEEDS

Short Fiction:

- A GROVE OF MOUNTAIN ASH
- A WALK WITH GEORGIA
- AN ALIEN ADVENTURE
- ASTROMANCER

- Because of the Christmas Stroll
- Beneath and Beyond
- Deep Dreaming
- Delia's Decision
- Egg Thief
- Enchantment, Inc.
- God-Touched
- Ice Storm
- Incident on the High Line
- In Search of a Valentinian
- Izzie
- Jolly Well Done
- Keystrokes & Intuition
- Miss Bainbridge's Christmas Party
- Miss Bainbridge's Summer Adventure
- Needle-Green
- New Year
- Opening Her Eyes
- Remembrance
- Silver-Tipped Death
- Simon Says
- Sisters in Suffrage
- Skye Dreams
- Spinning
- The Tie That Binds
- The Trail Where We Cried
- The White Dragon and the Red
- To Dream of Flying
- Treasures
- Trial on the Trail
- Wakinyan's Valley

"WDM Presents" Anthologies:

- Spun Yarns Unwound, Vol. 1
- Spun Yarns Unwound: Vol. 2
- Spun Yarns Unwound: Vol. 3
- Spun Yarns Unwound: Vol. 4

PREVIEW: ABDUCTED!

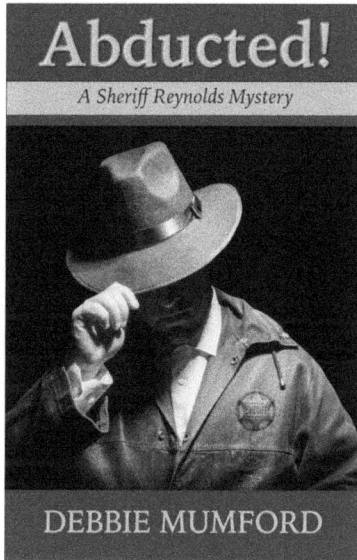

If you enjoyed this book, you may want to read *Abducted!*, the first *Sheriff Reynolds Mystery*. Here's a sample:

———

Sheriff Jason Reynolds strode into the single story white stucco building that housed the Garnet County Sheriff's Department. Nodding to the deputy on duty at the high wooden counter that separated the public portion of the room from the area where his staff worked, he headed for the door to his office.

Closing his office door behind himself, he glanced around the small room. It wasn't much to look at— a little on the dingy side, with pale green walls, an old-fashioned teacher's desk, a pair of gray metal filing cabinets, and an overflowing bookshelf— but it was his and he was proud to occupy it. Proud to be trusted enough by the citizens of Garnet County, Montana to hold this elected office.

Taking off his official Stetson cowboy hat, he hung it on the coat rack beside the window. Moving to his desk he settled into the ancient rolling desk chair and pulled over a stack of paperwork. Sometimes he thought the forms and reports bred in his inbox overnight, like oversexed rabbits. Sighing, he got to work. He loved his job, but he preferred solving crimes to writing reports about them or balancing the department's too often tight budget. Still, he had a good staff and a team of fine deputies. When they put reports on his desk, it was his duty— and his privilege— to read them.

———

Look for *Abducted!* at your favorite online retailer.

ABOUT DEBBIE MUMFORD

Debbie Mumford specializes in speculative fiction (fantasy, paranormal romance, and science fiction) as well as mystery and historical fiction. Author of the popular *Sorcha's Children* series, Debbie loves the unknown, whether it's the lure of space or earthbound mythology. Her work has been published in multiple volumes of *Fiction River*, as well as in *Heart's Kiss Magazine*, *Amazing Monster Tales*, and many other popular anthologies. She writes about dragon-shifters, time-traveling lovers, and detectives—whether amateur or professional—for adults as <u>Debbie Mumford</u>, and science fiction and fantasy for tweens and young adults as <u>Deb Logan</u>.

Join Debbie's special announcement newsletter list and receive a FREE story!

To learn more, visit Debbie at:
debbiemumford.com/
Or send her an email at:
deborah.mumford@gmail.com

facebook.com/DebbieMumfordWrites
amazon.com/author/debbiemumford
bookbub.com/authors/debbie-mumford
x.com/deborah_mumford

Milton Keynes UK
Ingram Content Group UK Ltd.
UKHW040306181024
449757UK00005B/359

9 781956 057287